Dispassionate Lies

Eileen Schuh

Wolfsinger Publications   Security, Colorado

"The real question is not whether machines think but whether men do. The mystery which surrounds a thinking machine already surrounds a thinking man."
~ B.F. Skinner

What Others Have Said About Dispassionate Lies

"This is a beautifully written novel with some complex themes. I found Dispassionate Lies to be a page-turner. Schuh is a fine writer and this is just another perfect example of her craftsmanship with a pen (or laptop!)"
~Suzy Turner, best-selling author of *The Morgan Sisters* series and *The Raven* saga

~ * ~

"An alternative world based on current facts by the author of sci-fi thriller Schrodinger's Cat and other novels; a satisfying and surprising ending to a story of intrigue, love and lust, and a woman coming of age in a most satisfying way. Give this book a chance—it will surprise, titillate, and fascinate you with current and futuristic scientific facts and emerging sensations scattered through-out the pages of this sci-fi thriller."
~Kenna McKinnon, author of *BIGFOOT BOY: Lost on Earth* and *Spacehive*

~ * ~

"Dispassionate lies is a brilliant lyrically gifted work that will keep you on edge from beginning to end. It follows the life of Ledesque a young and brilliant computer operator working in crime prevention and internet security. She works with an agency that subcontracts with other agencies including the FBI and the Canadian government; however, the book is only indirectly about her role as a computer worker. The book is about sexuality and governments and corporations attempts to suppress/expand sexuality—hers in particular.Ms. Schuh is a gifted writer. The book keeps you guessing and the twist at the end brought a smile to my face. Certainly worth the read. We live in an age in which the deepest and most complex parts of what it means to be human will be explored. Her writing kidnaps the reader and compels them to read more."
~Joseph Cautilli, Ph.D, Co-author of the *Zombies vs. Robots Trilogy*

CHAPTER I

The world was depending on her; she had promises to keep.

"Pssst, Ladesque!" Roach peered around his monitor as she entered the computer centre, his bright blue eyes sparkling. "I've made an amazing breakthrough."

It ought to be me, not Roach, making amazing breakthroughs. Several feet shy of his desk, Ladesque stopped. "Tell someone who cares," she grumbled. Immediately, a deep dimple appeared in Roach's chubby chin, enhancing his boyish look.

She plodded past him, settled into her steno chair and flicked on her computer. It groaned and her monitor sizzled as if the entire system was upset she'd disturbed its slumber. Impatient with the decades-old technology that ought to by now have been instantaneous, she drummed out a rhythm on her desk. It was actually more than just a rhythm. She'd learned American Sign Language years ago from a deaf playmate and often used it to talk to herself. *'I need a breakthrough,'* she signed. *'A breakthrough.'*

Her computer dinged, undoubtedly asking for her permission to do something. She ignored it. With a slight tweaking of programming even 2010 technology could be forced to look after itself. And she'd done that slight tweaking—a trivial success considering her much larger mandate.

'Breakthrough, breakthrough, breakthrough.' So far this morning, it was just her and Roach in the room. Even Porter, who was usually the first to arrive, hadn't wandered in yet. Alongside her and in front of her, a dozen vacant workstations waited for their people. The open-office milieu, the bosses said, was designed to encourage team work, enhance cohesion and increase communication. However, in her opinion, putting techies in an office without walls did nothing but encourage immature behaviour.

Working against the motion of the chair rollers, she entwined her legs beneath her thighs in somewhat of a lotus position. She wasn't as flexible as she ought to have been. She'd been rushed this morning and chose to sacrifice her daily yoga to charcoal mascara and champagne eye shadow.

Ladesque leaned forward, hoping to catch her reflection in the monitor. She'd been told often that she had her mother's eyes. She shared her mother's dark, thick, wavy hair too—or had her mom worn hers straight? *She's only been dead three years; I can't believe I don't remember.*

Ladesque quickly checked the family photo on her desk. Her mother's hair had indeed been dark and wavy—before the cancer treatments had stolen it from her. And her Dad's, thin on the top and greying—just as she remembered. Not until both her parents' smiles again felt familiar, did Ladesque look back at her monitor.

She caught the glint of Roach's silver pendant and felt the tickle of his breath on her neck. "I'm serious about my amazing breakthrough," he whispered. "Come see." He gripped the back of her chair, spun it to face his desk and began racing with her across the room.

"Stop it!" she protested.

Unable to get her feet to the floor, she grabbed at Porter's desk. Her fingers slid ineffectively along the smooth mahogany until she finally got a grip on the corner. The abrupt change in momentum wrenched her chair from Roach's grip and sent her spinning. On the first revolution, her arm hit Porter's desk organizer. A stapler and a dozen pens went flying. The second time around, her shoulder walloped his computer, stopping her chair dead and sending his monitor to the aging carpet with a thud and a tinkle.

Before she could so much as gasp, Roach had caught the back of her chair again and was shoving her toward his work station. He halted in front of his computer, plopped into his chair and began typing.

Ladesque rubbed her shoulder and peered behind her. Porter's monitor was strewn across the floor—sharp-edged chunks of metal and glass entwined in a labyrinth of cords and wires. A tiny spark crackled deep in its housing, followed by a puff of blue—like a last breath.

Roach slapped her arm. "Look!" He jabbed at his computer screen.

Ladesque untangled her feet and stood. "I just killed Porter's monitor and it's all your fault!"

"Never mind Porter's monitor. He wanted a new one anyway." Roach's hands brushed the keyboard. "Watch me make history!"

Ladesque hesitantly stepped toward the mess. "We could've started a fire and burned the whole place down."

"So what? Everything is backed up off site. Sit!"

"I can't believe you said that!"

"What did I say wrong?"

"The end of the world wouldn't matter to you as long as your fricken-ass data is backed up!" She stomped back to Roach. "I could tell you North Korea launched a nuclear missile, and you wouldn't care because your data is safe."

Roach slowly stood and faced her. "I didn't know Korea launched a missile. When?"

Frustrated, she slammed her fist against his desk so hard the sting traveled from her hand all the way to her aching shoulder. Roach continued staring at her expectantly. "Korea didn't fire a missile," she said between clenched teeth. "It was an 'if'. If Korea—never mind. I have work to do."

"You didn't say 'if'!"

"You're an idiot."

"Sit!" Roach roughly pushed her into her chair then took his seat and crossed his arms. Ladesque would've struck back if the man had looked anything like an adult. However, Roach had the demeanour of a younger brother—someone perhaps a grade or two past middle school. His push was like that of an exuberant child playing tag on the playground. She sighed and crossed her arms to match his. The entire tenth floor labour force was in its thirties. She was the only one who acted it.

"Watch the monitor," he said.

The screen was a blank white page at first. Then words began to appear. Faintly. Ladesque squinted and leaned forward.

"I've come here today," she read aloud, *"to explore with you the nature of the universe. Are you ready?"*

"Yes, sir," Roach said quickly. "I am ready. Proceed."

"I don't have time for this shit," Ladesque said.

Roach reached back and caught her forearm. "Watch!"

"You have a question?" appeared on his monitor.

"Yes…yes. A question…" Roach's fingers tightened around her arm. He leaned forward and spoke to the monitor. "What is the meaning of life?"

"Let me go, you idiot!" Ladesque wrenched free from his grasp and stood.

"Life is a process—"

"Don't you get it?" Roach asked. "It's God, communicating with us via my computer."

"Roach…"

"No, look, Ladesque. I'll put my hands behind my back. I am not keyboarding, yet words are appearing—"

"Roach!"

"It makes sense, Ladesque. Electronics is a fabulous way for spiritual beings to communicate with us. Our computers are harnessing the pure energy of electrons—quantum particles that transcend physical nature. Beyond matter. Beyond Newton's laws of physics. Existing on a purely spiritual plane—"

"Quite literally, for *heaven's* sake, stop. I'm not a moron."

"Are you saying I am?"

"Well, you sure as hell ain't God!"

"Could you at least play along with the illusion? There's commercial potential here. We could start our own church—"

"I don't want to start a church!"

"Think of the tax breaks."

"Roach, this is not the 1900s. This is decades into the third millennium. Where the hell are you going to find people who will believe God is talking to you through your computer? This generation knows magicians don't cut ladies in half. This generation, for years, has both mentally and physically interacted with video games. This generation doesn't even believe in God. And besides, how are you going to come up with words that sound anything like godly wisdom?"

Roach sank into his chair and scowled. "You're no fun."

"Here's a question for your deity," Ladesque said. "Dear God, what was my mother's maiden name? Game's over Roach. That simple."

"Nobody would ask God what their mother's maiden name is."

"Guess what? I just did and God couldn't answer. I wonder why, you idiot." She flung her chair in the vague direction of her desk, stepped over the remnants of Porter's monitor and stomped toward the exit. *I don't belong here.*

"If you were to ever get the internet back up and running like you promised," Roach called after her, "the program could secretly Google that maiden-name question and come up with a correct answer!"

"Ladesque!" Talon, the office director, called from three doors away. Ladesque glanced up at the surveillance images on the ceiling monitors. The slightly over-weight but always exuberant Talon was grinning and waving at the camera in his office. He jabbed at the phone on his desk. "A call for you!"

"Who is it?" she mouthed.

"I can't hear you! Come pick up."

Ladesque took a couple of steps toward his office then changed her mind and turned to the bank of windows. Ten stories down, traffic was insane. The world was not supposed to have turned out this way. And it may not have if the fallout from the global financial collapse that began in 2010 hadn't halted science and technology like no other event in history—except, perhaps, the ice age that sent Europe into the Dark Ages.

People were supposed to have had personal jet packs for commuting by now, or better yet, been able to work from home. She doubted that would ever happen, even if by some miracle she did get the internet up and running again. Man was a social critter, an animal who ran in packs. A colony of desperate, moving, seeking, working ants. At least from ten floors up, that's what her world looked like.

"Ladesque! Take the call, NOW!" She finally relented and proceeded to Talon's office. He was the only tenth floor employee who had his own space.

Talon motioned to the phone. "For you." Ladesque was positive no one had dreamed landlines would be back in vogue twenty-odd years after the first iPhones stormed the market. It was one of Ladesque's priority projects to develop the security necessary to enable the world to once again go wireless and digital. "It's the FBI," Talon said.

Ladesque strode past Talon. "The FBI, yeah, right." Talon had the best office in the entire building. Not only did it have a corner window overlooking the roof garden, it also had a five-hundred-gallon tropical fish tank—complete with real coral.

"It *is* the FBI," Talon insisted.

"Why don't *you* take the call?"

"They asked for you."

"They asked for me?" Ladesque tapped the aquarium.

"Don't tap the glass!" Talon shouted. "Can't you read the sign? It says, *'Don't tap the glass.'*" A clown fish wandered over to kiss her finger through the pane. "Yes, they asked for you. Answer the damned call."

"The FBI asked for Ladesque?" She tapped again and attracted a second fish.

Talon sighed loudly. "Yup."

"You lie." She reached for the jar of fish pellets and shook some into her hand.

"I'm not lying."

"You're lying again—by saying you're not lying."

"How do you know who they asked for?"

"Talon, who is Ladesque? Is that my name? No. Is it a name anyone beside you idiots call me? No. Is it a name the FBI would call me? No."

She sprinkled the fish food into the aquarium and watched the flurry of activity. Some fraternities had frosh, some initiation. Some men's clubs even had hazing. The tenth floor had nicknames. One did not belong, she was told, until one was given a nickname—preferably a nickname one did not like. She had no idea how her coworkers had come up with the name 'Ladesque'.

Initially she'd thought they were making fun of her Canadian heritage, since Americans thought all Canadians spoke French. La…La desk. 'La' since she was the only female, and 'desk' because that's where she stayed while the rest of the nerds gathered around someone's locker to drool over the latest porn magazine. La Desk—that's what she thought it was until someone wrote it on the assignment board. 'Ladesque', a meaningless word that appeared in no thesaurus. Meaningless, like her. Like her life.

"Oh, yeah," Talon said. "You're right. That's weird. How would the FBI know we call you Ladesque?"

"They don't know. That's my point."

"The FBI *did* ask for Ladesque."

"I'm not an idiot." She had twenty bucks riding on the bet, like all the others. It was somewhat like the vintage Seinfeld contest except it wasn't the last one to masturbate who won the pot but the last one to accept an assignment from the FBI. The temptations were considered equal since it was notoriously difficult for a computer nerd not to be seduced by the FBI.

"I'm not kidding," Roach insisted. "This has nothing to do with the contest."

The contest was to enforce the tenth floor's pledge to never help the FBI again. Ever. The geeks were protesting the fact the FBI constantly used their expertise but never gave them any public credit.

'*Our experts were able to...*' the FBI often announced at news conferences. The tenth floor wasn't the FBI. Didn't get paid by the FBI. Never even got visited by the FBI—phoned maybe, but for sure those surly agents in dark suits and reflective glasses would never actually set foot in the nerd cave and press the flesh of a binary expert. Talon said it was because they were afraid they'd catch some intelligence which, Ladesque had pointed out, was always what the FBI was after.

Talon had collected a stack of FBI media releases that said things like, '*France has asked the FBI for high-tech help...*' and '*Russia is calling on the FBI's computer expertise to help solve this issue...*' On the bulletin board in the coffee room was a headline clipped from a newspaper that read, '*The International Monetary Fund credits the FBI with South America's booming economy*'. Ladesque guessed Talon had pinned it there since he had headed the South American recovery project.

The tenth floor didn't deny the FBI dismantled the South American drug cartels but without Talon's business and political acumen, there would have been nothing to replace the lucrative drug trade that had driven the economy for decades. In fact, without Ladesque's efforts to destroy the cartels' underground communication networks, the FBI wouldn't even have been able to achieve the little it had.

"You take the call, Talon," Ladesque suggested. She tapped the glass again. "Or are you too afraid you can't say no to them?"

"They want *you*, I swear."

"Don't swear. Roach might hear you and he thinks he's God today."
She turned to leave.

"They've been on hold for you forever, Ladesque. I have to tell them
something."

"Tell them I'm in the can." Ladesque swept a pile of files off Talon's
desk as she strode past. "We are supposed to be a paperless society."

Talon picked up the receiver. "She says she's taking a shit...No, I don't
know how long she'll be. Women take forever in the can, especially when
they decide to go paperless..."

Ladesque tried to slide into her workspace without Roach noticing but
his eagle eyes caught the movement. "Why don't you like working here
on the tenth floor?" he asked.

"Because I have to." In the outside world it was a given: if one was
stuck in one's job out of necessity, enslaved to it for whatever reason,
one couldn't like it. However, on the tenth floor, nobody cared that their
life forever would be ten floors up from the pavement in downtown
Boulder, Colorado. From the moment the criminal background checks
were completed, the fingerprints and DNA taken, the personality profiles
completed, the oaths of secrecy signed, employees were enslaved to the
tenth floor. Forever. Such job security appealed to the geek natures of
most who worked with Ladesque. To her, though, it certainly didn't. Not
anymore.

"Everyone has to work somewhere," Roach protested.

A month or so ago, Global had even started random medical testing
on employees. She hadn't appreciated being poked and prodded just
to ensure she had a desk on the Tenth Floor in perpetuity. "This is a
workplace of idiots. Children in men's bodies."

"You're not in a man's body." Roach whistled toothsomely despite the
fact he knew his attempt at appreciation would enter deaf ears and was,
quite possibly, illegal.

Ladesque was asexual, a member of what the media had dubbed the
'eunuch' generation. Upward of twenty-five percent of North American
females her age were infertile and lacked libido—an unexpected result
of generations of chemical birth-control. Pill-guzzling and patch-crazy
females had stolen not only fertility from their female descendants, but
sexual desire as well. With the affliction so common and the victims
so accepting, asexuality quickly vanished from medical journals. It was
no longer considered a sexual dysfunction and was enshrined in the
constitution as a sexual preference.

At the age of thirteen, after she'd had her pheromone production
and pheromone receptors and preceptors tested, Ladesque attained
the official status of asexual. The diagnosis granted her special legal

protection and social benefits. It was also why those who'd hired her assumed she would function quite well amidst the male testosterone that dominated the tenth floor. Unfortunately they'd neglected to consider that sexual proclivity was just a tiny part of what separated men from women. Now, she was stuck here forever—with idiots.

"Why do you say this is a workplace of idiots?" Roach asked.

"You have to ask? You, who pretends he is God and expects me to believe he is? You, who insists upon being called Roach when your mother gave you a perfectly fine name. You who insists on calling me Ladesque when my parents named me—"

"Hey, there are valid reasons for the use of nicknames."

"Give me one."

"Same reason gangsters give themselves names like 'Tiny' or 'Scar Face' or 'Mama Boucher'—to disguise their identity from the cops, to separate themselves from their evil deeds and to protect their families from their criminal cohorts. We are, after all, top-secret workers working top-secret projects. Anonymity is important for the safety and security of not only ourselves but the work we do. Once you leave this building, no one knows who Ladesque is. No one can sue you for anything done here. No one can trace illicit tenth floor activities to your humble abode in the suburbs. No one can blame you—"

"What the hell?" Porter yelled from the door. He marched over to the pieces of his monitor strewn across the floor. "Who did this?"

"Sally Jergens," Ladesque said quickly.

"Who the hell is Sally Jergens? What the…" Porter kicked at the monitor and then bent to study its innards. "Wow. Cool. Ah ha. I see now how that works."

"I guess you're right, Roach," Ladesque said, returning to her keyboard.

CHAPTER 2

Ladesque went through the evening ritual of staring into the wall cam, sliding her card through the machine, and pressing her thumb onto the elevator button. Most didn't know, but she did—the elevator button read fingerprints. Apparently retinal and facial recognition technology didn't have her boss's total trust. That wasn't unusual. Since the tumble of the web, no one trusted high-tech. The metal door slid open and she stepped into the elevator that would take her directly ten floors down.

Global Construction Ltd. was the name of the company for which she worked. If it was named to disguise the nature of the company, she thought it was a poor choice. Global had to be the only construction company in the entire universe that didn't have a ground floor office. It was a generic enough name, though. It went unnoticed in conversation and in print. *'Who do you work for?'* 'Global Construction.' *'Oh yeah, I've heard of them.'*

The elevator doors opened and she stepped into the lobby. It was probably a takeoff name for Global Reconstruction, because that's what the tenth floor did—reconstructed the economies, the communication, transportation, and sometimes political systems that collapsed in the wake of the 2010 crisis. Ladesque was revamping the internet, making it secure. Making it tamper-proof, beyond the reach of organized crime and terrorists and basement hackers. Talon tackled foreign affairs while Roach's incredibly complex computer models had been used to solve problems as diverse as stimulating the American economy and predicting tornados.

She sighed. Her work day was over. She was no longer Ladesque. She was Sally Jergens, heading to the suburbs with the rest of the downtown crowd.

"Ladesque," a man whispered behind her. She took three quick steps to centre herself in the stream of office workers filing onto the street. To respond to a name was to own it, and that mustn't happen this side of the tenth floor glass doors.

As she approached the revolving door, she sought the man's reflection in the lobby window. He was walking directly behind her, towering over her. Although his features were distorted by the undulating lights and shadows, it was obvious it was her he was after.

She stopped and his toes smashed against her heels. The crowd crushed around her and then stumbled past. She and the man were now an island in a flowing sea of humanity—an island centred in the security cam's feed to the tenth floor. Someone ought to be watching.

She felt a hard object press against her spine. "Keep going," a muted voice ordered. She slowly merged into the crowd again. In seconds she was on the street. Increasingly desperate to draw the attention of someone in Security, she headed in the direction opposite her usual route. However, half a block later with no help in sight, the crowd thinning, and the man still on her heels her nervousness edged toward panic.

She had to take a stance, now. Statistics showed if she left the scene of the abduction with her captor, her chances of survival dropped to nil. She stopped in front of the bridal shop and stared into the store window. His reflection was floating there in the glass, between the mannequins. The slope of his shoulders and the tilt of his chin was oddly familiar.

"Why didn't you take my call?" he asked.

The only call she remembered not taking was the one in Talon's office. "I was seeing to my bowels."

"We need to talk."

She recognized that faint accent—his words a little more drawn out than the average Coloradan's. She turned to him. His familiar dusky eyes were on her. His thick lips twitching, wanting to smile. All fear vanished but for some reason her heart continued racing. "It's you! Casper?" The stirring low in her belly was intense—like that moment at the top of a rollercoaster.

"Paul," he corrected.

She'd known Paul as Casper, one of a very few tenth floor employees who'd managed to escape Global Construction. She'd heard rumours the FBI had bought his contract and his oath of secrecy; and that his life-long commitment now belonged to them. Perhaps he was about to offer her the same chance.

He burst into a full grin. The feeling of anticipation in Ladesque's belly unexpectedly dropped to her groin and exploded. She hadn't known the possibility of leaving her job on the tenth floor would be this exciting.

"We must talk," he whispered. Although strict new laws prohibited a man from sexually harassing a eunuch woman, that legality didn't stop Paul from wrapping her fingers in his hand. Nor did it stop the feeling that was once again building between her legs.

A billboard atop a building across the street flashed blue down onto her face. "Chemical castration of women is a sin!" The eunuch women aroused passion in all but themselves, it seemed. Some conservatives said asexuality was God's punishment for sexual liberation. Some said women who used the pill went against God's command to reproduce and their children's sterility was His revenge. To some, depriving females of their sexuality was a barbaric government plot designed to enslave them to the work force. Others insisted eunuchs were the happiest and most well adjusted females on the planet and proved women don't need men. Some scientists said it was a natural evolutionary process necessary to curb the earth's burgeoning population. Others said it spelled the doom of the human race.

Ladesque, along with the other asexuals, neither understood the passions eunuchs aroused nor desired to understand them. Despite the noticeable absence of asexuals from the debate, protective social institutions were established and laws were passed. It was now the legal right of asexuals not to want sex or children. It was illegal for anyone to discriminate against them or to pressure them to desire otherwise. And whatever support, counsel, education, or representation they needed was out there for them—free.

Paul still had her hand and took up stride. She had to scurry to keep from being dragged along. Reportedly, big industry liked eunuch employees because productivity increased when the labour force wasn't thinking about sex, had no reproductive commitments, required no maternity leave and never had to rush home to sick children. People whispered it wasn't human rights issues but rather eunuchs' value to commerce that drove legislatures to order their specific protection be written into law. She wouldn't doubt they were right—after all, recovery from the global recession was tough sledding.

She stared down at Paul's fingers entwined in hers and then glanced over her shoulder. The sin was not that they were holding hands, but that Paul had initiated the touch. There were surveillance cams everywhere; somebody must have seen. She wondered if she could play her eunuch card to get off the tenth floor. Maybe the FBI liked eunuchs, too.

Ladesque's mother had enrolled her in several early-intervention courses to prepare her for an asexual life in a sexual adult world. She'd been taught she was not a freak. Women had long ago mastered the ability to form strong non-sexual relationships—starting with their parents, siblings, and offspring. Women had always made close female friends, cared for animals, and enjoyed the company of gay males. She was told she could look forward to a life that included touch, kisses, and caring. There was no reason, she was told, she could not be passionate about other human beings, or events, or employment opportunities. If she wanted, science could arrange to produce for her a child to love.

Despite the training, Ladesque was never able to fully understand society's obsession with the sex drive, the pornography that fed it, the violence it initiated, the mating rituals that surrounded it. She did not experience hormonal mood swings, did not feel her biological clock ticking and could not find the humour in ribald jokes or whispered innuendos—despite the lessons, the videos and the Seinfeld reruns. She did know, though, she ought not to be strolling down the street hand in hand with a man. She once again glanced back.

Paul stopped. "Looking for someone?"

"Tenth floor security is supposed to make sure I get on the train safely. Apparently those responsible have become irresponsible—which is only human, I suppose, after watching a thousand people stream onto the street and head home, day after day. Week after week. Year after—"

"You're bored with your job," Paul interrupted. "I can help you with that." He had an even, strong voice, confident yet kind.

Facial symmetry was said to define the human concept of physical beauty. She looked up at his face—nicely trimmed brows arched over identical dark oval eyes. A well-shaped nose was centrally placed between two chiselled cheekbones. His ears were balanced, as were his lips and his smile. He would be considered very attractive by those who felt attraction.

He reached for her other hand and raised them both to his lips. The fleshy suction against her knuckles felt odd. "I can help you with lots of things," he whispered.

CHAPTER 3

"The FBI has offices in a textile factory?" Ladesque asked. From high above the workshop floor, she surveyed the bolts of fabrics, the robotic weavers and the vats of dye. Repatriating the textile industry to North American was one of the tenth floor's successes. It had been Roach's project and as far as she knew, nothing nefarious had been involved that would warrant the presence of the FBI.

Paul dropped her hand for the first time since taking it and leaned over the catwalk railing. He definitely had the appearance of a proprietor taking stock of his factory.

Ladesque looked from him to her hand which was quite warm because, she surmised, it had been cradled in another's for almost an hour. The fluorescent lighting glinted off the tiny beads of moisture pooling in her heart line. The padded parts were red and engorged—indicative of contact with heat. She wiped her palm on her pant leg.

"I have an interest in textiles," Paul said. He turned and stared into her eyes. "Among other things."

Ladesque quickly shifted her eyes to the floor. She'd been taught to read the body language of sexual behaviour. Paul had definitely held his gaze longer than was indicated for business or casual conversation. He was being passionate about something and it likely wasn't the breezy conversation they'd been having. Perhaps he had a passion for fabrics. Perhaps he liked her azure silk blouse, the way it came alive in the light, swaying and flowing and frothing.

She peeked up at him. He was still staring at her. That likely meant it was the curves beneath the silk that had him aroused. To protect herself from victimization, now was the time she was supposed to forcefully reject his advances.

But she didn't want to. Paul might have the key to her release from tenth floor drudgery and idiocy. No harm could come from giving him what he wanted.

On the other hand, if her desperation was palpable perhaps Paul was bribing her—offering her a new job in exchange for sexual favours? What if she obliged, only to find his vague promises were empty? Would he go home tonight a proud man for so easily seducing a eunuch?

"I've made you uncomfortable," he said. "I'm sorry. It's just that—never mind. Let me show you to my office."

She tried to keep her feet planted to the floor. Tried to open her mouth to protest. Tried to shake her head, no. She'd been taught that unscrupulous things could happen in private offices when sexual chemistry kicked in.

However, he again had her by the hand and she was willingly following him across the catwalk, away from the noise and the work below, into the shadowy hall. The thought of not being a virgin when she went home tonight was strangely exhilarating even though she obviously she had no physical need for sex.

She told herself the butterflies in her belly were just the result of anticipating the resolution of her curiosity about intercourse. She'd see a man as she'd never seen one before. She'd be able to confirm if a male in rut was as vulnerable as she'd been told and if the woman with him, held power—and if she had a new job in the morning.

The slight dizziness was from the height, from the long walk. It had been hours since she'd last eaten, it was likely just low blood sugar.

"Are you okay?" he said, swiping his card to unlock his office. The sign on the door said 'Paul Krimmons, Director'. She wondered what it was he directed.

He swung open the door and motioned her to a chair. Bright sun sparked off his polished oak desk. Two antique bookcases stood full and proud against the pea green walls. Paul walked to the window behind his desk, jammed his hands in his pockets and stared out at the weathered rooftops surrounding them.

Ladesque was struck by the symmetry of his stance as he stood silhouetted against the evening sun. While a woman's beauty was coiled in her curves and softness, the attraction of a man lay in his bulk and his lines. Paul's lines were perfect—straight broad shoulders tapered to a firm waist. Matching butt cheeks wrapped tightly in stretchy black cotton—

He turned abruptly. "You're staring at my ass," he accused.

Ladesque quickly averted her eyes and covered her hot cheeks with her palms. "I was just analyzing." The thought that he was going to totally misinterpret her behaviour, deepened her blush. "Analyzing your symmetry," she desperately continued.

Amusement lit his face. "Did I score well?"

"Symmetry of physical features defines a man's attractiveness—or so I've been told."

Paul cupped his butt cheeks and gave them a squeeze. "Apparently that is something you agree with?"

"I can detect beauty! Even be attracted to it—just not in a sexual way. You know all that. You worked with me for five years." Paul sank into his office chair, leaned way back until his face was tipped to the ceiling and then he closed his eyes. *I've rejected him sexually. He's likely trying to conceal his hurt or anger. The best thing to do is change the subject.* "You said you have a job for me?"

"I'm re-thinking that."

"Please don't!" Ladesque realized her swift response made her sound too easy and eager, but she couldn't stop. "I'm stifled on the tenth floor. I can't stay there."

He slowly opened one eye and peered across his desk. It was as if he was winking at her—but not quite. "I believe it's a felony to try to get out of your Global contract." He inhaled deeply and righted his chair, both eyes now wide open and on her.

I'm pretty sure I can give him what those sensual, delicious eyes are asking for—if that's what it's going to take to get off the tenth floor. "Just because I have no sexual desire, it doesn't mean I'm not able to have sex. I can't carry a pregnancy, but other than that…So, if you want…" His face was registering shock. "My parts are all there," she ended hurriedly.

"I'm not asking for your parts! For Christ's sake, for someone who is supposedly asexual you sure seem to be focussed on the damned subject."

"*I'm* the one focussed on it? It was you who grabbed my hand. Brought me into your secluded office. Kept your eyes on me far too long to be a casual glance. You—"

"I also told you I'm interested in textiles and I have a job offer for you. Yet those subjects didn't seem to elicit a similar eager response from you."

Ladesque set her elbows on her knees and cradled her jaw in her hand. "I'm sorry." She looked down at the peach-coloured cultured ceramic tiles that dated back to the 1980's. This was an old building. "I misread your body language and your intentions. Despite all my training, it happens. I've been taught to be observant and keep safe—"

"How does offering me your body parts keep you safe?"

"Sex generally isn't dangerous. I was told females often offer up their body parts to get their way."

"It's called prostitution."

"Not always. Sometimes it's seduction. Sometimes marriage."

Paul leaned forward and locked his eyes on hers. "That's not what sex is to me. Mutual pleasure and sober mutual consent makes the experience a pleasant one. Don't offer me your body again until you meet that criteria."

"I'm embarrassed." She glanced at the exit and wondered if she'd be able to find her way through the maze of corridors and stairwells back to the street. "I apologize profusely. It's best I leave." *I have no choice.* She rose and headed to the door.

"It's not a good idea to just up and walk out on me."

"Why not?" Ladesque wrapped her fingers around the cool nickel doorknob.

"It's against several laws to seek other employment when one is under contract to Global Construction. As an agent for the FBI, I would be compelled to report what transpired here today."

"I wasn't seeking other employment—I was offered it."

"A simple job offer doesn't negate your obligations to Global."

"But it was the FBI that offered it!" She turned to him. Paul was grinning at her, triumphantly. "Was all this just a set up to test my loyalty to Global?"

He shrugged. "It might turn into that."

"*You* entertained a job offer before escaping Global! How is my situation different from yours?"

"I didn't offer anybody the use of my genitalia during negotiations. I believe that makes my experience quite distinct from yours."

"As an asexual, I will be forgiven for misinterpreting our meeting. Besides…" She turned the knob and flung open the door. "Nothing would make me happier than getting fired from Global."

CHAPTER 4

Relieved to be miles away from Paul, Ladesque hurried up her front steps, punched in her security code and opened her front door. Lights came on and curtains closed. "Good evening," the robotic female voice greeted. Ladesque stepped into her foyer and shut the door. *Damn, it's a lonely life.*

At times like this, she understood why a New York Times reviewer made the controversial decision to put the best-selling *Eunuchs Make Good Friends* on the fiction, rather than nonfiction list. He said data proved eunuchs sought solace in suicide—not friendships. He said the book was a politically-sponsored attempt to get society to accept eunuchs into their hearts and lives, and thereby preserve the best work force America ever had. He said a generation unable to reproduce was hanging its way to extinction while readers devoured titillating, fictional, eunuch stories that smelled like a hymen and hinted at repressed desires.

The reviewer's eunuch daughter was purportedly among those who had lost their lives to suicide.

There was truth to what he was saying—those with any kind of sexual preferences seldom made lasting friendships with eunuchs. Partnerships between sexuals and eunuchs often crumbled abruptly—catching asexuals by complete surprise. 'Let's just be friends,' ended many pairings, as the sexual partner plunged into a new relationship that offered what the old one couldn't. It seemed to Ladesque that despite the intense public awareness campaigns, too many people still assumed if one had no sexual feelings, other feelings were muted and useless and eunuchs' broken hearts didn't hurt.

Though never spoken of in the media, it was a well-known whispered reality that eunuchs living with eunuchs often signed suicide pacts.

Ladesque's self-help group said the most successful living arrangements for eunuchs were those that involved female family members or small pets. Unfortunately, Ladesque had no living relatives. She'd been orphaned two years ago when her father's untimely death had quickly followed her mother's from cancer.

She opened her fridge. *I shouldn't have chosen stainless steel appliances—they add to the sterility in my life.* It was becoming painfully obvious to her that despite the assurances she'd been given, nothing highlighted the importance of sex in intimate adult relationships more than the lonely lives of asexuals. *I should have chosen a warm harvest gold.*

She pulled out the packaged tray of pre-washed veggies with hummus dip and ripped off the cellophane. Behind her, the fridge whooshed closed.

She might opt for a Pomeranian. They apparently were capable of unconditional love, were very forgiving, greeted you with unbound enthusiasm—day after day, and were sensitive to the emotions of their owners. They survived fine in city houses. It would be great to have something besides a robot voice greet her when she came home.

She dolloped some humus onto the veggies, plucked a napkin from the holder, and voice-commanded her TV to turn on the news channel.

Life sucked. Even more so today after embarrassing herself so thoroughly. She'd ruined her chance at a new job and put her current one in jeopardy. She tried to remember the clause in her contract outlining the fate of tenth floor employees who abdicated or got booted. She believed it entailed 24/7 electronic monitoring of all activities. With her technical expertise, she'd likely be able to bypass a good portion of that surveillance. It wouldn't, however, make her life any more pleasant. She'd be a watched woman forever…and a eunuch to boot.

Undoubtedly, she would be denied any opportunity to use her high-tech training, her computer skills, her smarts. With or without a Pom, her future looked very grey. Just as she sat down to eat, the doorbell rang and the speaker kicked on. "Ladesque, it's me. Paul. I need to apologize."

Her heart leapt at the thought of Paul's symmetric body gracing her living space. She studied the image in her brain. He would stand before her tall and strong. His eyes would be dark and soft. It was a beautiful image, sensual. She decided the reason sweat was trickling down her cleavage, her breathing was quick and shallow and her throat, tight was because she was distraught by loneliness and excited to have a visitor. And, she was hoping his job offer might still be on the table.

She voice-commanded the door to open and rose to greet Paul. He stepped in and was instantly more beautiful than she'd imagined. Beneath the mellow light filtering through chandelier crystals his features were firm, his lines strong, his angles accentuated by the shadows.

"I hope you accept my apology," he said. "I embarrassed you without reason today. I didn't know. I thought—" He stopped abruptly.

"What did you think?" Ladesque moved like in a dream toward him. Something heavy and full weighted her pelvis. She needed to—

"I didn't realize how brainwashed you are."

Ladesque stared at him. "Brainwashed?

"Your asexuality—"

"You're insinuating I'm the way I am simply because I've been brainwashed? That's coming close to denigrating my sexual preference—"

"Then, I must apologize again."

She motioned him into the kitchen. "Have a seat. I'll be with you in a minute." She headed down the hall. She had to pee. Urgently.

She wiped herself. Something was not right. It wasn't urine on the paper but something slippery and clear. Things below felt hot and swollen. Perhaps it was an infection, yeast maybe. Itchy. That must be why she wanted to rub.

She stared into the toilet bowl as she jacked up her pants. It didn't even smell like urine. It didn't have the sweet smell of yeast, either. It was…a warm smell. Thick and warm. She placed her hand on the crotch of her jeans and pressed. She could feel the dampness through the denim, the fleshy heat, the craving for more and harder.

She rushed to the sink, ran cold water through her fingers and splashed some on her face. *This is not supposed to be happening to me! Not now. Not ever. Never.* Perhaps it was a fluke. A hormonal anomaly. She'd have to ask her group. Had it ever happened to anyone else?

She walked awkwardly down the hall to face Paul. Her jeans fit too tightly—she had to widen her stance. He was sure to notice. Her face flushed. He glanced briefly at her and then returned to the magazine he was reading.

Grateful his eyes were occupied, she slipped in across from him where her supper was waiting. "I accept your apology, Paul, and I apologize for *my* actions. I read the situation wrong. I did not follow the protocol for social behaviour that I've been taught."

"What protocol would that be?" He squinted at the page as if deeply interested in the article on the Arctic meltdown.

"For starters I should not have let you whisk me away from the down town core. However, I did know who you were so that wasn't really a severe breach of protocol. On the catwalk, though, when you kept your eyes on mine for too long, that's when I should've said my goodbyes.'

"Why didn't you?"

"I need out of the tenth floor. I desperately need out of the tenth floor. I want the job."

"Is that the only reason?"

"Yes," she said firmly, although things below were still wet and engorged. He raised his brows, in obvious disbelief. "I know that it is against protocol on all levels to offer sexual favours in exchange for… anything. It just…it didn't seem like a big deal to me. It's not that I have an aversion to sex, I just don't have…the…desire."

"You're curious about sex?"

She shifted uneasily. "Yes. Yes. Curious. A bit. A bit curious. You're staring at me again. You shouldn't do that!"

"Why not?"

"It's…a…breach of…protocol…. Insulting."

"It's nothing sexual. I'm studying your reaction. Assessing your honesty. You are not good at lying."

Ladesque blushed. She wondered if he could hear her pulse racing, smell the swelling in her groin, see her nipples erupting beneath the azure silk. She wound her arms around her breasts and slid her chair forward until her lap disappeared beneath the table.

He slapped closed the magazine and pushed back his chair. "You do realize I can't tell you anything about the job I'm offering until you commit to it?" His eyes strayed to the TV monitor.

"In entertainment news today," the announcer said. The camera broke from the studio to a bride in a flowing white gown, reaching for the hand of a tuxedoed male. *"Canadian eunuch, Tracy Spence, author of Eunuchs Make Good Friends, married football star Avery Sell in a full-fledged church ceremony in the ornate Christ Chapel in Los Angeles. Spence born in—"*

"Turn up the volume," Paul requested.

"Here's Avery, explaining the male role in a union of an asexual female with a heterosexual male…" The video skipped to the tanned face of legendary quarterback, Avery Sell. *"Marriage is not about sex but about two adults committing themselves to each other. It is about respect, and bonding…About love that transcends the physical world…"*

The picture flipped back to the anchor desk, but Paul's eyes remained glued to the screen. "Where did they say she was born? Rewind it!" he ordered.

"Why?"

"Please." Paul glanced at her at then frantically back to the TV.

Ladesque tossed him the remote. "You do it."

He began replaying the clip. *'Spence, born in Montreal moved to LA—'* "Montreal, as I thought," Paul muttered as he fast-forwarded to the chapel scene and zoomed in on the bride. Her large luminous eyes were pasted to the eyes of her groom. Her pastel lips were curved into a soft smile. Her skin was fresh and smooth. A few golden curls spiralled free of her bright diamond barrettes and kissed the sandy rouge highlights on her cheek. Her face was very symmetric.

Paul zoomed in more and hit the hi-resolution button. The lady's eyes filled the screen. Metallic pinks and mauves sparkled beneath her brows. Thick black lashes, top and button, cradled a set of oval blue eyes. He hit a button and the screen returned to the live newscast. "Lust," Paul whispered.

"Phizenhessen Pharmaceuticals stocks soared today," the anchor said, *"following yesterday's announcement of the successful development of a non-hormonal oral contraceptive…"*

"What did you say?" Ladesque asked.

"She's in love with the man." Paul was still squinting at the image that was no longer there—his fingers tight around the remote.

"Yeah? So?"

He slowly set down the remote and turned his gaze to Ladesque's face. "She's a eunuch."

"We can still love, Paul. We aren't psychopaths. We have the full range of human emotion other than those involved in procreation. We—"

"She wants to procreate!" Paul interrupted. "Don't you see the passion in her eyes? And Avery—he's lying about it being a sexless relationship, I can tell. There is very much going to be a honeymoon tonight!"

"Whatever," Ladesque said. "I'm really not at all interested in others' bedroom activities. If they want to screw—"

"She's a eunuch!"

"Maybe she's been lying about that! She's been making her living by promoting eunuch-hood….Speeches, books, appearances…workshops. She's always seemed a bit too passionate about dispassion for my liking!"

"What about you?" Paul's eyes drilled into hers. "Have you ever felt the physical desire to procreate?"

"No!" she said quickly. She slipped her hands under the table to cover her crotch. For whatever reason, the excitement behind her pubis seemed sinful—as if she'd been living a lie for thirty-plus years. As if she'd been pretending she was something she was not. As if her career and life were based on a falsehood she was somehow responsible for perpetuating. As if she was about to break a bond of sisterhood.

"I've been trained to tell when people are lying," Paul said. His chair squeaked against the tiles as he rose. She felt his eyes on her but she would not, could not look up at him.

"You're Canadian, aren't you?"

"Yes."

"Born near Montreal, Ms. Spence's home town?"

"I was born in Kanata, Ontario."

"Is that anywhere near Montreal?"

"Different province. Frick, please don't do that American-thing and ask if I know her! Do you have any idea how big Canada is? It's twice as big as the States."

His eyes slowly dropped from her face, to her chest, to her lap and then back to her eyes. "Do you always lie?"

"Well, maybe not twice as big…" It was not the size of Canada that bothered him; she knew that but she wasn't about to confess to anything else. "However, it's huge, land-wise. Borders three oceans…" She wriggled uncomfortably. He was still scowling at her. He was a mind-reader. And persistent. "Yeah," she eventually conceded. "Kanata is near Montreal, just across the river. I wasn't lying, though, about them being in different provinces. The border runs between. What does all this have to do with anything?"

"Your mother, did she tell you anything about—never mind."

"About what?"

"About…" He hesitated. She could swear his cheeks were colouring. "About what to expect, perhaps?"

"Expect?"

"I can't believe this," Paul muttered.

"My mother's dead, what does she have to do with anything?"

"I know about your parents' deaths. I did a background check on you. But there must be someone. Do you have a sister? Aunt? Grandmother?"

Ladesque shook her head. "I have no family."

"Did your Mom have a close friend, a confidante?"

"Other than Dad, not that I know of. I left Kanata right out of high school and moved down here to take Computer Sciences at the University of Colorado. I wasn't home much after that."

A look of sympathy, or perhaps worry, replaced his scowl. "Your mother was Alice Jergens, correct?" Ladesque nodded. "I don't recall, did she have a maiden name?"

"Crate."

"You were a millennium baby, born in 2000, same as Tracy Spence." He sounded as if he was about to unleash a secret, but he didn't. "Check into it, Ladesque," was all he said as he turned and headed to the door. "I'll let myself out. Your job at Global Construction is safe for now. Return to your office tomorrow."

With Paul gone, Ladesque felt lost. Before he'd rang her bell, she'd intended to spend the evening scouring ads for Pomeranians. Now, though, all she wanted to do was cower under her duvet. The sensations heating her groin were not lessening. They were persistent, distracting, devoid of reason, and in need of resolution.

She found the number for her support group, picked up the phone and then, as if it burned, dropped it back in its cradle. Her lack of a sex drive had never been embarrassing. The opposite, however, was quite unsettling.

She suddenly understood why her mother had pined for the internet five years after the Great Crash, when it could no longer be denied government, corporate and criminal hackers had completely destroyed it usefulness. It would be fantastic to be able to anonymously search for medical journals, blogs, and newspaper articles with information on cases like hers—if there were any cases.

Also out there, hidden somewhere, was information on the connection she had to a Montreal-born eunuch celebrity.

Her support group met in two days, she'd wait until then before speaking about anything to anyone. She couldn't drag her thoughts from the feelings below. Her body mind and emotions persistently swirled around the physical longing. She'd heard cold showers would dampen the obsessive passion.

CHAPTER 5

"Ladesque!" Roach called as she slunk to her desk. "Did you know King Charles owns this building?" She took a noisy slurp of her coffee and hit the button to wake her computer. She had to get the persistent and never-ending security kinks worked out and get the world back online... and it had to happen soon. She'd made promises. This time unknown Black Widows would not be allowed to spin the web; cyberspace would not be free and ungoverned and ill-understood by those in power.

Internet technology lay fragmented and basically unused other than for entertainment—and even then, users were cautioned to protect information. Banks, media, governments, utilities, transportation, and retail still waited offline for her fix. She was into year two of the three-year estimate she gave her bosses for establishing a secure system. However, even though they'd doubled that to take into account the political steps that would be needed, she was far behind where she should be.

Her monitor blinked to life. "You're an idiot. I highly doubt the King owns this building."

"Did you flunk out of the contest last night?"

Her face immediately reddened at the thought of the Seinfeld contest. She was glad her back was to Roach. "No."

"You left here last night with the FBI."

"How the hell do you know?"

"Spiker from Security told me."

"Why wasn't Spiker downstairs making sure I got safely on my train?"

"He said you didn't look like you were in any trouble. Said he had to grant you privacy. Said it appeared you wanted to leave with the guy."

"Bullshit! I stopped right in front of the surveillance cam over the exit door."

"But then you left—"

"Yeah, because the idiot had a knife to my back!"

"Really?"

"Not really, but he might have. He was pressing something into my spine."

"His hand, maybe? Gently caressing your lower back—"

"There was nothing gentle! What was I supposed to do? Confirm the type of weapon being used before obeying?"

"There was no weapon."

"How do you know?"

"Spiker said Casper is harmless. Talon agreed. Said you leaving with an FBI agent might hurt your contest chances, but it wasn't exactly a dangerous situation."

"Spiker and Talon knew it was Casper?"

"We all knew it was Casper. So, did you lose the contest?"

"Did you have anything to do with the FBI leading me out of here by the hand?"

"Me?" Roach asked, overly innocently.

"You bastards! You were all watching me on video, weren't you? You thought if you let me go with Casper, I'd give in to him and lose the bet. Talon and his fish tank were in on it, too, weren't they? I can't believe that you idiots would put my life in danger just to win my twenty dollars!"

"You lost?"

"No, I didn't lose! He didn't even ask for my help."

"What did he ask for?"

"My mother's maiden name."

"No, seriously, Ladesque."

"Serious."

"Did you give your mother's maiden name to him? Because if you did, I think that means you helped him and you ought to pay up."

"You're an idiot, Roach."

"I'm not an idiot. Do you believe in dreams? Last night I had this terrible dream that unbeknownst to us, the entire tenth floor has always been working for the FBI. So, this morning I had a buddy of mine run a title search on this building. It isn't the FBI that owns it, but the King. Do you think that means we're working for Britain?"

"What do you mean, the king owns it? The property title says King Charles on it?"

"It says it's Crown property."

"Oh, for Christ's sake, Roach. That's just a legal term. It's probably the Canadian government that owns it. In Canada, government property is said to belong to the Crown. It has nothing to do with King Charles."

"Oh. Do you think we're working for the Canadian FBI?"

"There's no such thing as the Canadian FBI."

"What about the Canadian CIA or Homeland Security?"

"CSIS."

"I don't know much about Canada, but it came out of the recession first, didn't it?"

"It never really went into a recession."

"Why?"

"Canadians were on top things, perhaps. Educated. Computer literate.

We knocked down organized crime the moment cyberspace began to fail. I remember learning in school that in 2010, law enforcement efforts began to topple the Montreal underworld…" Her words sparked memories of Paul's interest in Montreal…and her mother.

"And?"

"I—I don't know. I was only ten. Forget it." Something more important than the dismantling of the Mafia and the Hells Angels had happened in Montreal back then and after what happened last night when the lights went out, she fully intended to discover what it was.

Archived copies of pre-depression internet activity, salvaged from various clouds, computers, and web servers, existed in the tenth floor vaults. She'd spent an entire year creating programs to safely scan the trillions of digital cyberspace files and eliminate the corrupt ones. Although many files after 2010 were too corrupted to be useful, she'd saved what she could and designed software to disable any threats that were still active or lying in wait. Then, she'd spent another year figuring out how to safely store her 'scrubbed' files in a useable format. She couldn't guarantee she'd totally bleached out the marks of the Great Crash hackers, but she could guarantee no insidious evils were still active in the files.

That's where her successes ended. The breakthrough design she needed to protect both her scrubbed files and future cyber-data was proving elusive. So far the only security system she'd come up with was keeping her scrubbed files under lock and key.

"Perhaps Canada is stronger than the politicians admit," Roach prattled. "Perhaps this is their building, we are their workers, the FBI is at their mercy. I mean, if they weren't hit by the recession, perhaps Canada rules us without our knowing. Or, maybe they were behind the Great Crash and are holding the rest of us hostage. I'll bet King—"

"Are you anywhere near finished with that secure satellite programming? I won't be very popular if dial-up is the only internet option I can present to the world."

"Even if you're right that it's not King Charles' who owns this building, isn't it odd the Government of Canada owns an office tower in Colorado?"

"Yes, it's odd. If we were to get the damned internet working maybe we could find out why." She'd been led to believe she was working for the U.S., but perhaps she was working for her homeland. Perhaps…but she'd likely never know for sure; that was one of the pitfalls of holding a top-secret position.

What she did need to know for sure was why her mother, Montreal and eunuch Tracy Spence figured in the files of the FBI.

It took a few hours of cajoling before Talon granted her permission to lock herself in the vault with the ancient web data. She'd lied about her need to access the files, knowing she wouldn't have been allowed to use company time and hardware to search her personal history. She had little time to feel guilty, though. Finding out what link she had to Tracy Spence and Montreal was rapidly becoming an obsession. On the pretext of malware research, she plugged in the necessary hardware, flicked the right switches and settled into the chair. A few passwords later and all things Canadian in 2010 were laid out before her.

There was much less coverage of the global economic collapse on Canadian news sites than on European and American sites. It was as if Canada stood to profit from the ailing economies elsewhere. Recurrent headlines included stories about the strong Canadian dollar—on par with or above the US dollar after decades of being much lower, new technology making the paper currency almost impossible to counterfeit, and the dismantling of The Hells Angels biker gang and several other criminal organizations.

Then there was the saga about Russel Williams, the Colonel who had become enslaved by an escalating sexual passion for silky women's underwear. He attacked several women and murdered two before being caught. Ladesque's remembered being taught the sexual wiring in the human brain often got short circuited. Intense sexual feelings could arise from pain, fear, shame, and anger. Although fantasies arising from these rogue connections were usually played out safely in the bedrooms of the nation, sometimes the urges became so strong the seekers of pleasure took their fantasy into the land of the real.

Paedophiles found children arousing. Necrophiles desired sex with dead people. Voyeurs loved to look. Rapists had an insatiable need to dominate their mates and Colonel Williams liked silky underwear, stealing silky underwear, wearing silky underwear, and eventually killing for silky underwear.

Ladesque shivered. She remembered the night after Paul's visit. The all-consuming heat raging between her legs had not gone away but rather had intensified, stole all thoughts, and begged for satisfaction. No wonder the world was in chaos when a force as unpredictable and as powerful as sex was governing human behaviour. No wonder moralists blamed all things evil on sex.

Cyberspace crimes also dominated headlines in late 2010—from a viral attack on a computerized Iranian nuclear power plant to the grounding of F-35 jets because of computer malfunctions which, judging by the way the story read, were a result of sabotage.

Surprisingly, Ladesque found no news stories anywhere in her files that linked the cyber madness to the economic crisis. It was remarkable those in the know were able to keep the wretched state of the internet such a total secret for close to five years, even with the high-tech communications available at the time, the thousands of self-proclaimed e-journalists, and both Snowden's and Wikileak's penchant for publicizing e-secrets.

Ladesque searched the files for her mother's name and found her listed as a scientist at the McGill University Human Sexuality Research Centre in Montreal. Excited to find such a strong connection to the hints Paul had dropped, she leaned in and began rapidly searching key words.

Ladesque had only ever known her mom as the warm person always around to prepare meals, tidy the house, smile and offer a hug. Unless her search yielded more results, her mom would never be more to her than that distorted childhood memory.

She tried finding her mom's web page, or email, or a blog—but surprisingly her search netted nothing. The Alice Jergens she knew was not on Facebook or twitter or any of the other social and business networking sites that were popular at the time. At least, she wasn't participating under her own name.

Ladesque was about to plunge into a search on the Human Sexuality Research Centre when her watch alarm beeped. She couldn't stay late because her eunuch support group was to meet after work and later in the evening Paul was coming over, hopefully with a more concrete job offer.

Eager to find out if anyone in her group had any information on what was happening to her down below, she hurriedly erased her tracks, consigned the information she'd learned to memory, and stowed the hardware in the safe.

CHAPTER 6

"This entire thing makes me feel like a second class citizen," Mabel complained. Mabel was always complaining. In Ladesque's opinion, if the woman were to drop a hundred pounds, she'd be happier. "I don't know why my sexual preference or lack thereof is anybody's business but my own."

There were six of them gathered in Marielle's living room, sprawled on black faux-leather sofas that harkened back to the start of the century. The late summer sun streaked in through the picture window, hit the plants and furniture, and slapped long shadows onto the laminate floorboards.

"It *isn't* anyone's business," Sheila jumped in. "And that is why your rights are enshrined in law. To keep it from being anyone else's business."

"Think about what you're saying, Sheila. In my humble opinion, law books and law courts have no place in my bedroom, either. Sex, or lack thereof, is not a legal issue. Protect the young and vulnerable if you want and outlaw violent and non-consensual sex, but for Christ's sake, I'm an adult. I don't need lawyers protecting my vagina!"

Ladesque giggled, imagining a pod of lawyers at the foot of Mabel's bed with their swords drawn and their shields ready.

Sheila sighed. "I'm just not into this entire political thing. All I know is that the older I get, the more emotionally vacant my life seems. Pomeranian kisses are nice, but..." She rested her chin in her hands and gazed out the window at the silhouetted skyline.

"We can't miss something we've never had," Mabel said.

"Rumour is our Miss Tracy Spence not only loves, but lusts. Is that possible?" Ladesque asked.

"I never trusted that bitch," Mabel said. "She's worse than politicians for publicizing our personal affairs."

Ladesque straightened. "Has it ever happened to anyone that...I mean, historically, have female eunuchs ever become sexually aroused?"

Everyone in the room stared silently at her. "Like in dreams or anything?" she continued. "I read that people with spinal cord injuries can still experience mental arousal even if their bodies..."

"Hmmm, Sally," Sheila said. "If you're talking eunuchs, no. By definition, no."

"I just wondered if sometimes things might change or something..."

"Has it happened to you?" Mabel asked, suspicion lacing her words.

She narrowed her eyes and wrinkled her brow. "Do we have a traitor in our midst?"

"I was talking about Miss Tracy," Ladesque said quickly. She turned from the group to set her wine glass on the end table and conceal her blush.

"You're sure about that?"

"Very sure," Ladesque said, her cheeks still burning. She ran her sweaty palms down her pant legs.

"Sally," Marielle said. She slid open the patio doors and beckoned to her. "I want to show you my bougainvillea." She closed the glass doors behind them and pointed to the spiny vine lacing itself through the white metal railing.

"It has white bracts!" Ladesque exclaimed. "I've never seen —"

"You're Canadian. Were you raised near Montreal?"

"Yes. I—"

Ladesque heard the patio door slide open behind them. "What are you two doing?" Sheila called.

"I've been in touch with Tracy Spence because—" Marielle whispered. "Never mind. Talk to your mother."

"But my mother is—"

Marielle turned and whisked toward Sheila. "I was showing Sally the white bougainvillaea." Ladesque noticed the absolutely perfect curve of Marielle hips beneath the brushed denim of her jeans. "The rest of you saw it last week." Two little gold pockets on her butt cheeks moved with her stride. She stopped in front of Sheila and widened her stance. Her thighs were firm and nicely curved as well.

Sheila was looking past Marielle to Ladesque, her breasts heaving beneath her thin red cotton sundress. She stepped aside and Marielle glided back to her guests. Slowly, slowly, with her eyes glued to Ladesque's, Sheila approached. Closer she came, her heels clicking on the deck, her hips swaying. The wind catching her skirt. She smelled good, better than the bougainvillea, sweeter than the yellow potted rose. Intoxicating.

"Don't let Mabel upset you with her rhetoric," Sheila said. "Many of us are curious about the sexual nature of mankind. It doesn't mean we are traitors to the sisterhood."

"I'm—I have no mother to talk to. I was hoping this group... Whatever."

"Depressing loneliness is slowly happening to all of us. Our siblings are marrying and becoming tied up with their young families. Our mothers are aging and losing their acuity. We see emptiness in our futures and wonder if we're missing out on something beautiful."

She was gorgeous, standing in the glow of the evening sun. The breeze caught Sheila's body heat and washed it over Ladesque. The woman's lips were full, flushed, and swollen. "Despite the rhetoric we've been dished, we've all seen the sadness in our mothers' eyes." Ladesque wanted to wrap her in her arms, press their lower bellies together, kiss those lips and feel past them, deep and deeper until she filled Sheila's empty place. "Sally?"

"I'm sorry." Ladesque dropped her eyes and kicked at the cedar decking. "I need to be alone for a moment. I'm missing my mother."

"Sure." Sheila backed up two steps and then turned and hustled into the house. The door slid closed.

Ladesque leaned on the railing and watched the sun sinking lower and lower. The days were becoming noticeably shorter; soon they'd be a lot colder, too. How was it that she'd gone so quickly from being asexual to being hyper-sexual? Everyone and everything looked delicious. And all she could think about was immersing herself in the heat and the glow, the promise, the desire, the anticipation. Rub and press and grind. Even the plant pots, the trellis…the newel post…She needed to reach that ultimate place toward which all things were streaming. She slipped down the deck stairs, crossed the lawn past the day lilies and headed home.

She'd just started up her walk when a vehicle pulled to the curb behind her. She was barely aware of it, so intently was she concentrating on the pleasurable sensations coursing through her body. They were uncontrollable, innate and self-centered.

She'd always imagined the sex drive to be a more magnanimous hunger—underwritten by a loyalty to one's species and a desire to procreate. She'd thought the desire would be discerning and guide one to seek a mate possessing desirable genes. For her, though, desire was distorting perception, making everything including plant pots seemed sexually inviting.

The car door slammed. "Ladesque?" Paul's voice rang out.

She turned. He was standing in the soft shadows of the summer evening, airbrushed by the faint orange of the flickering street light. He was chiselled and symmetric and positively gorgeous. Her eyes wandered to his crotch before she caught herself and forced them quickly to his face.

"Paul, you're a bit early. No?" Mutual consent and pleasure, he'd said. She was positive she could now meet his criteria. Unfortunately, the man looked as if he was on a professional mission. "I thought you said eight o'clock." He was wearing a dark suit, carrying an attaché case, and had a pen stuck in his breast pocket. "It doesn't matter. Please, come in."

He probably had no sexual attraction to her. Believing she was asexual, he would have assumed taking her hand would be seen as a simple gesture of friendship. When he'd stared too long into her eyes, he'd simply been sizing up her honesty and her suitability for his job, as he'd said. He'd more or less told her he wasn't interested. She ought to respect that. She had to. She had to quench her unrealistic desires. Somehow.

He followed her into the house, slipped off his polished oxfords and wandered to the kitchen table.

"Coffee?" she asked.

"Sure. De-caf." He set his leather attaché case on the table and clicked open the brass locks. He pulled out a beautiful chrome and black computer that sparked blue as it came alive. "The FBI thanks you for setting up our encrypted intranet."

"The FBI is welcome." She wondered if Paul had any idea of how much time and effort had gone into securing his bloody intranet. Plus, there was the ongoing intensive monitoring and maintenance to ensure it remained secure. That was the last project she'd done for the FBI before the contest clicked in. Ladesque flicked on the coffee maker and watched dark brew flow into the cups. It smelled delicious. Sexy.

"Can I assume that since you agreed to this meeting, you're on board?" He shrugged out of his jacket and hung it carefully on the chair next to him. He was wearing a wonderful periwinkle cotton shirt. Tailored pleats drew it across his broad shoulders and angled it down to his thin waist.

He settled into a chair and began tapping his keyboard. The wide collar, framing his neck, flattened and fanned into lapels across his upper chest. She was sure she could see solid pectoral muscles moving beneath his shirt as his fingers flew. It seemed to take forever before he realized she hadn't answered. He looked up at her quizzically. "You do want this job?"

It's not your damned job I want, can't you tell? Satisfied her lower half was well hidden behind the kitchen counter, Ladesque pressed her fingers to her crotch.

"Are you all right?" he asked.

There was a definite odour to arousal. She rinsed her hands under that tap and grabbed the two cups of coffee. "Do you take anything in it?" she asked. "Baileys, perhaps?" She set the mugs on the table, opened the liqueur bottle and gurgled too much of the sweet cream into each cup. She slid his to him.

He stared dejectedly at the steam rising from his mug. "You shouldn't have done that. I'm on duty." Which she knew also clearly meant she should not be imagining the two of them grinding their pelvises together. She wondered how the human species had managed to survive if this is what the sex drive was like. No wonder sex was ridiculed, laughed at, joked about, abused. The human species liked to feel superior to the world, more a god than an animal, denying baser instincts and needs like meat-eating and breast feeding. Yet, man was a prisoner to primal mating urges. What else to do, but laugh about it?

She sat opposite Paul and stared past him out the window onto the darkening street. For the first time in her life she was aware of the chair cushion beneath her butt. It was cradling her cheeks and following the contours of anatomy. Perhaps her sex drive was unusually strong, an unforeseen delayed side-effect of living in an environment rife with manufactured and genetically modified hormones. Perhaps, hers was a vicious rebound effect—after years of depleted pheromones perhaps they had burst forth abundantly—

"Are you okay?" Paul asked again.

"Yes." She wrenched her thoughts from her imaginings, set her feet firmly on the floor, and took a sip of coffee. She concentrated on the sweet scent swirling beneath her nose—caffeine, cream and alcohol.

"You seem distracted."

Distracted is not the right word. "Perhaps I had too much wine at Marielle's."

Maybe she was distracted. If Paul had approached her before whatever it was that was happening to her had happened, she would have had the nature of his employment offer figured out by now. With her genius and background and what she knew about Paul and textiles and from the snippets of info he'd given her, she could've concocted a pretty accurate scenario, if she had tried.

Instead, she'd been researching 2010 Montreal headlines, the Human Sexuality Centre at McGill University, Colonel Williams, and the death of Rizzuto, Canada's mafia king pin—killed in his kitchen by a single shot to the head. She'd been searching for the digital footprint of her mother—and she'd been dreaming about falling and flying and having sex.

"This is a bad time, then." Paul slapped closed his computer and yanked at his jacket.

"Please, stay." Ladesque quickly reached for his arm. "It will only take a few minutes for me to sober up. I'll make us something to eat. We can talk about other things for a bit. Really. I'm not totally hammered or anything. Just a little drizzled-out, as they say."

"Who says 'drizzled-out'?"

"I don't know—"

"I believe I told you I was coming. You were expecting me, right?" Paul halted his movement but his fingers still tightly grasped his jacket, ready to tug it off the chair and wrap it over his strong, square shoulders—"I presumed you'd be ready to talk business."

"I am, totally. You're a bit early, that's all. If you'd come when you were supposed to…" *If he'd come. If I'd come. If we'd come together.* Ladesque rose and dumped her coffee down the sink with a flourish. "See? I'm fine. Perhaps I'm just a little nervous and am trying to delay my decision. Can you tell me anything to set me at ease?"

She poured herself another coffee, this time without the Baileys, and rejoined him at the table. If she wanted to ever get off the tenth floor she had to get her urges under control. His scolding had definitely helped; her mind had cleared considerably.

"Ladesque, there's little more I can tell you about this job until you commit. I can, however, outline some of what your commitment would entail. You will…" He droned on about her security check and the release Global Construction would give her and the hours she'd be expected to work and all the verbotens. It was, he said at some point, a position that had the potential to launch her into a spectacular career.

The sun had set and with only the dim dinette nanobulbs lighting his face, his chiseled features were much softer—

"…and that's about it. So, are you interested in this job?" Paul asked.

Ladesque's mind shifted into high gear. Textiles—high-tech textiles. Perhaps as high-tech as metamaterials and nanomaterials. Top secret inventions or discoveries that were somehow related to computers and the internet, because those were her areas of expertise. Textiles, computers, nanotech…quanta. Quantum computers, perhaps? But none of that had much to do with the FBI's mandate to fight interstate and international crime. She'd heard rumours, though, and been privy to some of the FBI's more unusual requests of the tenth floor techies.

"I'm not going to be fighting interstate and international crime, am I? Perhaps there's been a secret shift in the mandate of the FBI since the global collapse?"

"Good guess. Our responsibilities have expanded dramatically since 2010. The government vowed to never again become a slave to a technology it doesn't understand. Putting the wealth and security of the nation in the hands of the anonymous computer wizards running the internet was a thoughtless act. Interstate and international high-tech crime-prevention is now a big part of our mandate. It was a lot less conspicuous and more effective to just add a branch to the FBI than to strike up a new organization. Lines of communication and authoritative structure were already established, checks and balances and security protocols were in place. Jurisdictional conflicts and rivalries were avoided."

"What else can you tell me?"

"What I'm telling you isn't top secret information, but it's privileged. Do you understand that?"

"You know that I, along with all tenth floor employees, have high-level security clearance."

"Sensitive information can normally be shared between those with high-level security clearance. However, you can't share what I'm about to tell you with anyone, no matter what their clearance."

"Gotcha."

"The FBI through its High Tech Crime Prevention branch, HTCP, is now mandated to monitor all technological advances, pinpoint where they are occurring, identify who is pursuing them, uncover the motives behind the research and development and discover the uses being envisioned. If necessary, we plant our own researchers in the labs so we can hold sway over the developments as well as collect intelligence. We mostly do this for American research, but we communicate closely with like-branches of INTERPOL and other such agencies around the globe. We do not want to be taken by surprise again."

Ladesque knew from Paul's lengthy and passionate response he was either a director of the FBI's entire HTCP branch or at least the leader of one of its high-tech teams. The prospect of honing the cutting edge of technology was thrilling. She'd be researching it, using it. Controlling it. She'd be powerful, off the tenth floor and…she'd be near Paul.

"Where do we go from here?" she asked.

"I'll prepare the employment contract and you will sign it."

"You can tell me nothing more before I commit?"

"How interested are you?"

"I'm very interested, but—"

"That's good enough for us to proceed. Everything you need to know will be spelled out in the contract."

CHAPTER 7

"You're sure you want to do this?" Talon asked. He had his feet on his desk and was chewing a pen. Ladesque walked to his aquarium and rapped on the glass. "For the last time ever, DON'T DO THAT!" He threw his pen at her as if it were a dart. She ducked but it pierced her shoulder, fell to the floor and rolled out of sight beneath the fish tank.

"Ouch! Yes, I'm sure I want to do this."

"It will cost you twenty dollars and your pride."

"My pride? I don't think so. I'll be so proud to work for the FBI instead of the tenth floor idiots." She turned to him. "It's worth twenty dollars. In fact, I'd have given you two thousand if it meant getting out of here."

"Global isn't hiring to replace you." Talon slid his feet from his desk. His chair fell forward with a clatter. "Your project's being put on hold."

"Are you sure? Who told you that?"

"The boss."

"When were you talking to the boss?"

"He called this morning to make sure protocol was followed re your quitting. You have to be escorted to your desk, all your passwords removed, your ID turned in, blah, blah, blah and la dee dah."

"Was he upset that I'm leaving?"

Talon stood, jammed his hands in his pocket, and walked out from behind his desk. "He sounded relieved, actually. He said you'd been stymied in your project for months and it wasn't likely you would meet the deadlines Global promised the international community for the return of the internet."

"Yet he's not hiring anyone to take over? Does that make sense?"

Talon shrugged. "I guess he figures if you can't do it, no one can. He's right." Talon wandered past her, grabbed the jar of fish flakes and dumped a lid-full into the tank. "We're going to miss you, Ladesque."

"You are?" She wondered if he had his back to her to conceal his emotions or a lie.

"Yeah." He sighed, slowly turned to her and raised and lowered his arms as if in defeat. His face reddened and he took a tentative step toward her. A quick shrug and he was coming in for a hug. It was all

Ladesque could do to keep from stepping away. His heavy hairy arms wrapped around her shoulders too tightly. His chin was too close to hers. His whiskers tickled her neck. And then, quite unexpectedly, his head was resting on her shoulder.

"Talon," she protested quietly.

He stepped away and rubbed his hands together nervously. "Sorry. It's just…the boss said to give you a warm farewell. To make sure you leave on good terms." Talon's cheeks again turned red. He skipped back to his desk, plumped into his chair, and swivelled to face the wall.

"You're serious, aren't you? You're going to miss me."

He kept his eyes on the framed certificates hanging over the file cabinet. "Yes."

She wondered what kind of relationship he thought they had. Men rarely viewed eunuchs romantically—or so she'd been taught. Some might take pleasure in the challenge of seduction and experience arousal at the thought of conquering virginity, but few would feel romance or even kinship or closeness and definitely weren't likely to be heart-broken when the relationship ended.

However, one couldn't predict the romantic behaviour of vastly insecure men—like the entire tenth floor labour force, who only ever dared to desire women they couldn't possible have and could thereby be safe from both rejection and commitment.

"You're going crazy, Talon. I suggest you find yourself a woman." Ladesque walked briskly out the door. She paused in front of the window to look down at the street for the last time. The worst part, perhaps the only bad part, of quitting was leaving behind the tenth floor vault with its archived copies of the 2010 cyberspace. She might never find out what happened in Montreal and what her mother had to do with it.

Ladesque sighed, wandered down the hall and into the office. She'd brought a small cardboard box to take home the few items that were hers—a family photo, her plastic name plate, a giant eraser 'for the big mistakes'. She walked to her workstation and tossed them in.

Immediately, Roach was beside her, opening her desk drawer. "I'll give you a hundred bucks if you stay." He grabbed a handful of Global Construction pens and threw them into her box.

"So generous," Ladesque muttered.

"Generous? The pens or the money?"

"Your generous help with my packing."

"We're going to miss you around here." Roach was staring at her.

She quickly looked away. She'd never felt close to any of these buffoons. She wished she'd known they felt something for her, that she'd been considered one of the pack, a member of the clan. That she'd held a special spot in their hearts. She'd have been significantly less lonely had she known. Had she felt she belonged somewhere, to someone. That people cared.

Roach was still staring at her. It was all too late now. At least she would be leaving with warm feelings, as mandated by Global's boss.

Roach's phone rang. He started toward his desk and then turned back, searching her face. "You'll be missed."

She glanced down at the meagre belongings scattered across the bottom of the box. "It's my understanding I was on my way out anyways," she said.

"I don't believe that!"

"Talon said the bosses didn't think I could complete the project I was hired to do. They're not replacing me."

"Only because you're irreplaceable."

"I'm serious, Roach. I think they're right. The project is at a dead end and I'm at a dead end. Time to move on." The phone quit ringing.

"You'll call? Drop by?"

"First thing I'm going to do is call with a request for tenth floor help. We'll see who is next to be kicked out of the contest."

CHAPTER 8

"Clean out your desk, return home, and wait for phone call from me," Paul had said.

Ladesque plunked her small box of belongings onto the kitchen counter and stared out at the city. Deep blue clouds edged in halo-white were climbing over the mountains, tumbling across the prairie, rolling towards her. Saying her goodbyes had been much tougher than she'd ever imagined.

She'd thought her tenth floor colleagues saw her as simply an embodied intelligence programmed to focus on binary codes and security breaches. An untouchable and unfeeling being ruled by a brain rather than a heart and groin. She'd thought her colleagues were societal misfits, bordering on insane.

But the truth was she was going to miss tapping on Talon's fish tank and miss even more his yelling at her when she did. She'd miss Roach's extreme efforts to impress her with his wizardry. She'd miss Porter's unabashed love for wires and buttons and toggle switches.

She'd miss her desk, looking down at the street from ten floors up, the direct elevator ride to street level. The security cams, passwords, thumb prints. The vault archives she'd never gotten to properly explore. Despite having read virtually the entire spectrum of cyberspace, in one form or another, she'd translated very few of the bits and bytes to English.

All her brooding abruptly ended when the phone rang and she heard Paul on the line. "Are you ready to get to work?" His words were well rounded, complete and laden with soul, as smooth and strong as his body. The inflection, perfect.

"I am," she replied.

"Please meet me at my office. You remember how to get here?" His words vibrated through the receiver and into her head. *His voice is electric.*

"Yes. Do I need to bring anything?"

"No, I'll show you your work space today and tomorrow you can bring whatever you need to make it your own."

~ * ~

Paul's office door was open when she arrived. He motioned her to close it behind her. She was instantly awash in new-found sensations—smelling him, seeing him, feeling the warmth emanating from his body.

It was a slow process settling in across from his desk, entranced as she was by the straight strict lines of his suit and the little curl on his forehead that had spiralled free from the gel. Not wanting to stare, she focussed on the name plate on his desk—brass imbedded in mahogany...embedded. In bed...Feelings were heating her face and stoking her heart.

He was not concealing the fact her unsigned multi-page contract was on the desk before him. "How much do I need to tell you about this job and how much have you already guessed?" Paul asked.

That he'd ask that question before asking for her signature, was unsettling. "Pardon?" *If I say the wrong thing, will that unsigned contract be destined for the shredder?*

"What do you think your job here will entail?"

Perhaps she knew enough to impress him; it seemed he was giving her no choice but to try. "I'm assuming I've been pulled off the Global project because my efforts to develop a breech-proof world-wide internet will all be for naught in the near future due to nanotechnology research sparking the invention of the quantum computer—a computer so powerful it will easily, in the snap of my fingers, over-power any security features I may dream up. Am I right so far?"

"You make it sound as if it was the FBI's decision to shelve your Global project. I need to make it clear, it wasn't. We don't make Global's decisions for them. They simply subcontract their expert labour force to us. We—"

"Stuff the bullshit, Paul," Ladesque said. "You're talking to a woman with an IQ past the two hundred mark."

"I'm not lying." He chuckled and Ladesque's heart melted. He looked even sexier when his features softened. A dimple appeared in his left cheek. It wasn't symmetric—he only had one. But it was a great one, offset perhaps by that curl twisting toward the other cheek.

Ladesque squared her shoulder. "In that case, it must be the Government of Canada that makes Global's decisions." She watched his face to see if she'd impressed him, but he was revealing little. "Decades before the Great Crash, Global Construction, a high-tech company under a different name, was founded. A Canadian company? Perhaps?"

The quick subconscious nod from Paul was all she needed to know she was on the right track. However, if she kept going, would she derail? *What does he need from me before I get to sign?* His continuing silence indicated she must say more.

She struggled to remember the historic headlines she'd skimmed in the vault the other day. She'd not read many business news items, as she'd been looking for stories about her mother and human sexuality. However, Roach's comments about Canada's role in the Great Crash had prompted her to read a story or two about Canada's war against organized crime. Several big businesses, owned by gangs to front their illicit activities, had tumbled during that war. One story mentioned the fear that was generated when it was revealed a high-tech firm headquartered in her home town of Kanata, Ontario had close links to a criminal organization. Since Kanata shared a common history with Boulder as a centre of high-tech, perhaps if she put the two together…

Against her better judgement, but melting under the intense pressure of Paul's lengthening silence, she continued. "Global's predecessor was originally owned by a criminal organization. The Canadian government acquired it when the courts designated it 'proceeds of crime' and confiscated the assets, which included intellectual property—"

"Who told you this?" Paul's poker face fell apart and tension creased his brow. He leaned toward her.

I've said the wrong thing. I knew I should've shut up. "No one."

"What else do you know that you shouldn't?" he asked, his confusion obvious.

There was nothing she could do but keep going. She cleared her throat. "To keep on the cutting edge of communication technology, Canada partnered with its US neighbour and surreptitiously bought into one of America's cyberspace hot spots—Boulder, Colorado, home of Google and IBM. It transplanted its tech company and renamed it Global Construction. That's about all I can tell you. I haven't figured out the politics of the situation or how the FBI fits into the scheme." Relieved to come to the end of her story, she exhaled and settled back.

"Who else besides me has been talking to you about these matters? Someone from Canada, perhaps?"

Ladesque's heart leapt. *Does he think I'm spying for my home country?* "Nobody told me anything. Honest." Paul's eyes drilled into hers. "I was in the vault, remember? Searching the old files. The amount of info the internet contained was amazing. I didn't tell you anything here today that wasn't public knowledge at some point."

He raised his eyebrows. "The surreptitious Canadian purchase of the Global building was public knowledge on the internet?"

"I found out whose name is currently on the building's title, which is public knowledge. Then I threw in a lucky guess."

Paul's eyes busily scanned her face. She surmised he was reviewing and assessing all she'd said. A half-grin slowly appeared. "I guess public knowledge without the politics is not very useful."

"It won't help me figure out my role here."

"You're asking me to fill you in?" He turned the contract to her. "Did you read the copy of the contract I gave you to review?" Relieved to finally have the chance to sign, Ladesque nodded and reached for a pen. "You understand it all? No questions?"

"Ninety-five percent of this contract is outlining things I won't be doing and the consequences of doing things I shouldn't." She began initially the pages. "There's hardly anything about what I *will* be doing."

"It's not a position that lends itself to a job description."

"*Duties include any or all of the following*," Ladesque read to him. "*Research and development, analysis, reporting, recommending, following up on recommendations…*"

"Important stuff. Not many people can wrap their head around new technology, let alone predict where it's going."

Ladesque stopped and pointed to a phrase under the duty, *Follow up on Recommendations*. "It says here, '*Addendums to this contract will be offered for signature should participation in recommended actions vary significantly from those included herein and should they entail untoward risks.*' What does that mean?"

"It means if your research and recommendations lead to places you don't personally want to go, you can opt out of the project—without risking reprisal. It protects us both. Because you won't be required to participate in something just because you recommended it, your recommendations will be more credible."

"For example?" Paul didn't answer. Ladesque stopped flipping pages and looked across at him. His fingernail was intently scratching at a spot on his desk where Ladesque saw nothing. "It will become clearer as we go along," he finally said. He stopped scratching, but kept his eyes glued to the spot. His apparent nervousness rattled her.

She returned her attention to the contract. "It doesn't say what happens should I refuse to follow up on one of my recommendation."

"You'd be assigned other duties," he answered quickly, as if relieved to have been asked an easy question. "You are highly skilled in a variety of areas. We'd certainly be able to find another spot for you."

"You seem bothered by this clause—"

"Not at all. Quite the opposite, actually. You won't be working just for me, you'll be working for the committee. This contract was carefully prepared to address all committee members' concerns. I fought long and hard to get that clause put in for you."

"Why?"

"Some members thought professionals at your level must be willing to stand behind their recommendations and wanted someone in this position who was willing to offer a full commitment up front. They expressed concerns that Skinner's—that some of our important projects might be in jeopardy if you were to back out after a certain stage. After all, the criteria used to select you for the position—never mind. It will become clearer. I'll tell you about some of the politics behind Global."

"That will make things clearer?"

"Some things, I'm sure. The Global building is viewed somewhat as an embassy." Ladesque listened to his smooth voice, as she worked her way through the document. "It is operating outside the laws of the US and under the auspices and legal control of Canada. This arrangement allows both nations to function independently and protect their own national interests and security while at the same time nurturing the symbiotic relationship vital to rebuilding the world economy. Sign here..."

Ladesque scribbled her name and tossed down the pen. "Sounds noble. Why all the secrecy?"

"Secrecy's a necessity; it ensures sensitive research data doesn't fall into the wrong hands."

"How secret will my role be?"

"Very."

"Am I that agent you plant in the nano factory? Do I anticipate the new security measures the world will need when metamaterials reach the public domain? Am I to thwart the research? Am I the developer of the quanta computer?"

"What role would you like to have?"

"I want to invent the quantum computer and unleash it on the world."

CHAPTER 9

Early October 2035

Ladesque plucked the family photo from her box of possessions, wiped her sleeve across the glass and set it on her expansive oak desk. Paul had assigned her a spacious corner office with windows all round— on the floor overlooking the textile factory. Her office opened into a private lounging loft, lit from above by a bank of skylights.

There was a suede chocolate-brown sofa long enough and comfortable enough to sleep on. Behind it on the wall, hung an expensive Persian rug. A glass-topped coffee table and brass floor lamp accentuated the décor. Defining her lounge, a border of a dozen potted jungle plants breathed life and freshness into the empty spaces.

She hoped her luxurious surroundings indicated Paul had forgiven her for being so flippant and unprofessional yesterday. *Why the hell did I say I fancied inventing the quantum computer and unleashing it on the world?* She'd simply meant the thought of masterminding and possessing such power gave her quite a rush, but she had the distinct feeling Paul had not liked her answer. *What if he thinks I intend to sabotage his reconstruction efforts and attack the world with quantum technology?*

Her present office milieu was a lush contrast to the usual setting of those enslaved to their computer obsession. The openness and comfort, options and isolation, were a bit overwhelming. She'd never before had the choice to sit at her desk behind walls, or lie back on a sofa and watch clouds through a skylight. Or wander over to the railing and look down at the textile robots two floors below.

She stepped out of her office and scanned the ceiling of the loft. There were sprinkler heads, heating ducts and blinking smoke detectors. She did not spot any security cameras. That was different as was the fact she was an entire staircase away from the nearest office—which was Paul's.

She heard his footfalls on the wooden stairs, muffled by the acoustic spray blanketing the steel girders and concrete walls. She ambled to the sofa and watched breathlessly for him to appear. It would be like having him in her house. She straightened a throw cushion. *It will be like having him in my boudoir.*

His head appeared about the floor boards. The moment he spotted her, a smile lit his face. "Settled in?" he asked.

She nodded. His shoulders appeared—square and strong, still draped in the dark suit jacket that marked his rank. His waist, belted with leather. A nondescript silver buckle—she quickly raised her eyes to catch his. "This is a beautiful space. Thank you."

He was walking toward her, a sheaf of official looking papers in his hand. Her knees gave way and she sank to the sofa. He stood before her, just off to the right, gazing down. What was it she saw in his liquid dark eyes?

He waved the papers. "Would you prefer we go over these in your office?"

Suddenly aware he'd been waiting for her to invite him to sit, she scooted over and patted the cushion beside her. "Here would be great," she said. As he approached, his crotch was even with her eyes. He smelled delicious.

"The FBI's High-tech Crime Prevention branch, works closely with other government departments," he said. "The military, NASA, and the CIA among others are heavily invested in the metamaterials research we are overseeing. Technically, the textile factory below is a private enterprise but they've been known to be unable to resist funding; government dollars have paved our way into their research projects."

Ladesque pointed to the railing that cordoned off the work floor below. "The dye vats and weavers are just a cover for high-tech government research?"

"Perhaps, but more like a fund-raiser. The factory runs quite efficiently and is well-known for its wonderful and unusual fabrics, which are actually commercially viable by-products of the research in the HTCP materials labs. The factory is our money laundering machine, so to speak—a legitimate private business both investing in and benefiting from something more covert—the HTCP materials lab. We learned the trick from organized crime. It takes a lot less paperwork and fewer votes in congress if we're funded by a business enterprise rather than by taxpayers' dollars."

"That's how Roach successfully repatriated the textile industry. He combined the lower labour costs of robotics with your research and development of fabrics. Voila! New products available only from USA manufacturers." She rose and wandered over to where she could watch the work below. The convoluted links between science, commerce and communication were mesmerizing. Business, dollars, government, espionage, intelligence…textiles and computers. She glanced back at Paul. He must be a genius to have so seamlessly woven all those threads into a tapestry that worked. He was staring at his papers on the table and clicking his pen against the glass. *I think he's annoyed I wondered off.*

While working on the tenth floor, she'd taken courses in appropriate work-place behaviour but had never had the chance to practice those skills. *I'll have to brush up because behaving in unexpected ways creates conflict in an organization.* She scurried back to the sofa.

"I'm sorry. There is just so much new information to integrate, an entire paradigm for which I was unprepared. I'm trying to wrap my mind around it all."

Paul shifted slightly as she sank beside him but she wasn't sure if he'd moved closer or farther away. "That's okay," he said. "However, I wasn't expecting you to think so deeply about these things. I intended this to be a quick briefing. Perhaps you could save your deep thoughts for later? I have another appointment in half an hour."

I'm pretty sure he moved away. Damn! "I apologize."

"I'll get quickly to your role in this scheme, then leave you to contemplate. Our lab is on the verge of creating sheets of flexible metamaterials. The cloak of invisibility these materials offer is of high interest to the military. Are you familiar with metamaterials?"

"In a nutshell, metamaterials are artificial materials engineered to have properties that may not be found in nature. These fabrics gain their properties not from the stuff they're made of but from their structure at a microscopic level. Negative refractive index designs have been created that alter the way sound and light behave around the material. Some, instead of reflecting light, bend light."

"Yes. We have the blueprint for a fabric that bends both the visible and invisible light spectrum. An object covered by it would not be detectable by radar, infrared detectors, night vision goggles, sonar. Until one bumped into it, one would not know anything was there."

"Yes, invisible but still of substance," Ladesque said. "That is, I couldn't walk through a wall wrapped in this material."

"No, but you could see through it—"

"The first commercial use will likely be in construction of massive buildings such as arenas. Concrete support posts could be wrapped in negative refractive index materials, giving fans an unobstructed view of the field from anywhere in the stadium. The posts, though invisible, would not have their integrity diminished in any way. They'd have to be cordoned off so people wouldn't walk into them—"

"I obviously didn't hire you to contemplate the safety issues surrounding metamaterials in construction. Think instead about the link to computers."

"Computers?"

"There *is* a link. Closely related to the metamaterial industry, is nanotechnology—"

"Nano—meaning very tiny," Ladesque cut in. "Nanotech deals with developing materials, devices, or other structures by manipulating matter at a subatomic level."

"Right. But—"

"The link between nanomaterials and computers is their use in electronics. If one could use the power and the characteristics inherent in subatomic particles—quanta—one would possess extreme power. Quanta can appear in two places at the same time, appear and disappear, be a particle, be energy. They have spins and flavours, and tops and bottoms. To date, computer systems have been powered by the binary system, all programming must be either a yes or a no, an off or an on. It's a lot of programming and is limiting. Hardware adaptations over the decades managed to increase memory and speed. As well, building on past programming allowed significant advances in software capabilities. However, quanta would add an entire new dimension to computers. It would add the maybe to the yes and no, the grey to the black and white, the half-way to the off and on. It would make a computer with a complexity similar to that of the human brain. But, is it possible to create such a machine?"

"Why not? A quantum computer wouldn't be the first time the power of the subatomic was harnessed. Aside from the atomic bomb, researchers discovered decades ago complex biological systems such as chlorophyll production and animal migration, make use of quantum mechanics."

It was obvious Paul was hinting the quantum computer either existed or was very close to being realized. Ladesque felt her excitement building. "Theoretically, a quantum computer would be able to do the massive calculations needed to unravel the mysteries of the universe, solve social problems, instantaneously unlock encryption—"

"Therein lies a problem, perhaps?"

Paul's words brought her down to earth with a thud. "I suppose keeping it secure might be challenging, as would keeping it under control. Who would decide who gets to run the thing? Maintain it? Have access to its power?"

"Those kinds of ethical issues would have to be firmly addressed."

"Those issues are a tad more than ethical, I'd say. A quantum computer would process information quickly, store it in immeasurable quantities, communicate it seamlessly. It would actually create information. It could be programmed to program itself, regenerate, evolve. It would, as it sits now, rule the world, untouchable. Unbreachable. Without rival." Ladesque grinned at Paul. "I want one."

"Whether or not you or anyone else gets one will not be your decision or mine. Try to keep your enthusiasm at bay and prepare a research paper on metamaterials, nanomaterials and quantum computers to present to the committee entrusted to make the decision. Outline if and when such things are likely to be created in usable form. Compare our research progress to others on the international scene. Speak on the likelihood of the potential uses and abuses, pros and cons. Should we proceed with research and development? Should we stop our research and prevent others from proceeding? Should we hurry with our work, wait and see, proceed in a different direction, build a defence against this technology rather than proceed with developing it, etc. etc. On your mark, get set…"

Paul rose. The cloudless sky peeping through the skylight over his head gave him a blue aura. "Go!" He turned his back and headed down the stairs. His feet, his legs, his torso, disappeared beneath the floor boards. He stopped and grinned at her through the railing. "Any questions?"

His smiled melted her. *I don't want him to leave.* "Just answers."

He chuckled and disappeared.

CHAPTER 10

End of October 2035

Ladesque was unaware of the comfortable couch or the refreshing palm trees. She did not hear the late-autumn rain pounding the skylights above. She didn't catch the whir of the textile factory below, immersed as she was in the reports and data, summaries, findings and conclusions of metamaterial and nanotech research.

Not until it was too dark for her to read, did she set the papers down, stand and stretch. Metatechnology had been on the verge of a breakthrough way back in 2010. Because the idea of cloaks of invisibility had been so enticing, research continued basically unabated throughout the collapse of the global economy and the crumbling of cyberspace.

Ladesque bent and switched on the floor lamp. The bulb glowed low and warm and then slowly began to brighten. From what she could see, some forms of useable metamaterials had been on the market for decades. However, useful negative reflective index materials were no closer to reality than they were three decades ago and nanomaterials would likely never hit the market. The nature of quanta was proving to be more elusive than imagined, more magical than previously believed, more strange, harder to harness.

"Quanta truly are the beginning and the end, the Alpha and the Omega" one scientist lamented. "The big bang and the final collapse. Everything and nothing—all at the same time."

"The deeper and deeper we look at the smaller and smaller," another researcher hypothesized, "the bigger and bigger it becomes until ultimately the singular building block of matter becomes the composite of all that ever was—the singular nothing from which all things burst forth at creation."

"Developing nanomaterials is like trying to flatten God into a sheet of tinfoil."

The thought of God sparked thoughts of Roach and his computer. Nanomaterials might be decades away from reality, but nanoelectronics weren't. They were here. Now. In several labs around the world. And the quantum computer was incubating—getting ready to hatch.

The God Machine some dubbed it, because it would potentially be omniscient and omnipotent, the creator, processor, and keeper of all knowledge.

Ladesque walked to the railing and leaned over. Two floors below, work continued. Robotic arms wove and dipped and dyed and threaded and rolled. Machines needed no sleep, no family time, no overtime. Innovative American textiles rolled out, 24/7.

The God Machine….The wall light in the staircase came on and Ladesque heard Paul's heavy steps ascending. His head peaked over the floorboards. "You ought to go home," he said.

She suddenly felt quite tall, looking down on him. The room around her shrank until it was just her and him and he was smiling, his dimple, deepening. His dusky eyes were washed in shadows and his hair was edged in yellow from the glow of the light behind him. He bounded up the remaining steps and hurried toward her. His unexpected speed caught her off guard.

Fatigued from hours of intense research and fearful of being tossed to the floor below, she quickly stepped away from the railing. Immediately embarrassed, she covered her face and giggled.

Paul stopped a few steps from her. "What's the matter?" Shadows from his brow shrouded his face in mystery. "Has something's scared you?"

She pointed lamely to the books and papers scattered across her lounge area. "I've been at it too long. This entire high-tech thing is scary."

"Scary? What's scary? To most of us, it's exciting."

"Because most of us don't understand. Or maybe we do but don't care."

"My people care," Paul said. "Believe me, Ladesque. My people care."

His voice, though quiet, was laced with intense passion. He tilted his head and his eyes came out of the shadows, deep and clear, holding steady on hers. "That's why you're here, Ladesque. To both guide us in our decision and to steer these developments in the right direction. Don't think you are just a figure head, a token expert to soothe our conscience. Your voice will be heard—" Although his inflection indicated he had more to say, he stopped abruptly and averted his gaze.

It's like he's holding something back, something less soothing and comforting than the spiel he just delivered. Perhaps she'd just been at it too long, weaving the past into the present and predicting the future and analyzing the ethics and all the potential uses and abuses. She'd felt so tall and powerful when Paul had first entered and now she felt anything, but.

Needing comfort, she wrapped her arms about herself and wandered back to the sofa. Probabilities, human nature, human history, the uncertainty principle, Schrödinger's Cat, Skinner's Box, and Everett's

Many Worlds Theory. The entire body of science from the past century was related, in one way or another, to quantum computers.

Still deep in thought, she rounded the coffee table and dropped onto the sofa. *Stephen Hawking's event horizons made invisible black holes appear, but figuring out how to make the visible disappear was proving trickier.*

She looked up. Paul hadn't followed her to the sofa but stood where he was, his head bowed, running an Oxford toe along a floor board. His shoulders drooped as if he was either weary or sad. Ladesque wondered if his demeanor was related to the secrets he was hiding.

It was quiet in the loft for several minutes as Ladesque returned to contemplating the depths of the universe and Paul—

"Let me take you to dinner," he said. Suddenly, her papers and books and thoughts about quanta and the universe disappeared. It was her and him, alone in her loft in the evening shadows. Her heart quickened, although it shouldn't have. Her boss was simply rewarding her for working late so many nights in a row. It was well into the evening, he was probably just hungry, as she was. On each side of her pelvic bone, beneath the tightness of her jeans, her pulse beat feverishly.

He probably had in mind a quick meal together, a drink to unwind, perhaps a bit of shop talk. *I must get my sex drive under control before it ruins my career, my life. My future.*

Paul was very obviously not interested in her...sexually. At all. Ever. Because he knew she was a eunuch. She could not afford to embarrass herself again, to offer him her body parts and be refused.

"Sure," she said. "Dinner sounds great. I'll get my coat." She tilted her head and stared at the skylights. "I believe it's still raining out there."

~ * ~

The waitress whooshed by, her lingering lavender perfume overpowering the scent of autumn rain emanating from Paul's damp shoulders. "Did you manage to get through all the information I gave you?" he asked.

Ladesque imagined Paul's lips on hers and his hand on her crotch—Dishes clattered in the kitchen and a rush of cool air swirled around her feet as another late-night customer entered. "Almost. I need another day. Some cross referencing..."

"Clue me in on what you will be recommending in your report." His lips were moist and smooth and full. She remembered when he'd kissed her fingers on the street in front of Global. The fleshy suction on her—

"Ladesque?"

She dropped her eyes to the table. "I'm sorry." She dipped four fries into the pool of ketchup on her plate and for some unfathomable reason, shoved them all into her mouth. She realized too late her tongue was much too dry to swallow them. She grabbed her glass of ice water and took a swig, trying to coax the water around the fries, hoping to lubricate their way down her throat. It didn't work; the fries simply dammed the water in her mouth. She was dangerously close to having it dribble out and down her chin.

"I'm the one who ought to be sorry," Paul said. Ladesque wondered if another wee sip would provide the pressure need to get the fries moving or if it would make things worse. "You're tired and hungry and have worked many more hours these past weeks than anyone in their right mind should expect. You definitely don't need shop talk right now."

Close to gagging and unwilling to suffer the humiliation of spitting out, she had no choice but to swallow. The water and most of the fries swept past her tonsils but a stray lump caught halfway down and burned into her oesophagus. She took another swig, and then another. Finally, when she'd drained her glass, the lump moved and the pain eased. She rubbed her throat and ran her napkin over her mouth and nose.

"Forget I asked about your report," Paul continued, "and tell me something about yourself that I don't know."

Something about me that you don't know? The burning dropped to her groin and she thought about rubbing there instead of her throat. *How about the fact that all I can think about is sex? Self-centred, self-pleasing sex…with you.* She shifted on the bench and covered her face with her hands.

"Are you finished eating?" Paul asked. "I'll ask for the bill and take you home."

CHAPTER 11

He was lounging on her sofa when she walked into work, his head propped on a cushion and his feet hanging over the arm. She stopped at the top of the stairs, surprised and abashed. It was like he'd moved in, uninvited.

He was reading her notes and didn't look up. She wondered if she could slip past him into her office and close the door between them. She didn't want a repeat of last night's dinner episode, that awkward moment when he pulled to the curb and reached for the keys but didn't turn off the engine.

She'd fumbled with her seatbelt and searched for the door latch. "I'll wait here at the curb until you're safely in," he finally said, ending the tension. "Catch up on the zee's tomorrow morning, Ladesque, and I'll see you at the office after lunch."

Now, here he was in her space, comfortably in her space. Reading her stuff. The boards beneath each footfall creaked ever so softly as she inched toward her office. "Ladesque," he said just as she put her hand on the doorknob. "We have to talk." He did not sound happy. She turned in time to see him glance quickly at his watch.

"I'm sorry I'm late," she apologized. "When you told me to sleep in, I thought you were serious."

"I was serious." Paul set his feet on the floor and tossed her notepad onto the coffee table. "I wasn't expecting you here this morning. Don't worry about that."

"What then?" Ladesque stared at the notes he'd been reading. She felt like someone had been snooping in her diary, even though she knew that since he was paying her to write, her words belonged to him. *I'm his, work-wise at least.*

Paul nodded to her papers. "You don't think it's possible to create useable sheets of negative refractive metamaterials?"

"Not in this millennium."

"No invisible cloaks? You're going to disappoint millions."

"They'll get over it, like the ancients got over the fact they couldn't turn base metals into gold."

"What's the biggest thing preventing this invention? Lack of money? Lack of knowledge? Gravity?"

"Man's inability to deal effectively with the inherent ambiguities of reality. Before we can successfully manipulate matter in its basest form, the human brain needs to develop to the point where it can analyze and integrate knowledge from across the spectrum of scientific specialties and comprehend the multi-facetted, contradictory, timeless nature of the universe."

"Do we have to wait for the evolution of the human brain or would a quantum computer do the trick?"

"I wasn't able to uncover enough information on quantum technology to answer that. In the past, it was believed computers were limited by the intelligence of those programming them. The quantum computer, though—perhaps if integrated with chemistry and biology...I don't know."

"You also nix the possibility of nanomaterials ever attaining commercial value. Tell me why in a way that will be understood by the committee."

"When quantum physics' secrets first got leaked to the public in a language the populace could understand, artisans and poets ran with the idea of Many Worlds, Schrödinger's Cat, time travel, chaos theories, and uncertainty. Physicists laughed at them, saying the laws of nature at the quantum level did not translate into the macro world; the actions and traits of electrons and photons and mesons at the subatomic level have no impact on us and our world."

"And then?"

"Then, somewhere along the line, scientists forgot that they had laughed and began believing as the artisans. They shouldn't have. Paul, we cannot bring the intangible into the tangible, the minute into the macro. Quantum laws and Newton's Laws cannot co-exist. As soon as a nanomaterial reaches macro size, it becomes, by definition subject to Newton's laws. For Christ's sake, it's simple...you've parked your ass on nanomaterial, Paul. That entire couch is made of subatomic particles. You threw my nanomaterial notes onto my nanomaterial coffee table. Our entire universe is made of nanoparticles, is constructed of nanomaterials—yet doesn't behave like quanta. That isn't going to change!"

"We're wasting our time and resources researching it?"

"Not necessarily."

Paul moved over and patted the sofa beside him. "Sit."

Ladesque eyed up the spot and then for reasons she was unsure of, curled into the recliner across from Paul. *I guess I have a better view of him from here and the view is...nice.* "Some of the metamaterials being researched have a brighter future, but it might take a decade or two to figure out how to commercialize them. In the meantime, mankind is gaining valuable information by pursuing this line of thinking and that could lead to things not yet conceived, just as alchemists made great scientific discoveries while pursuing their quest to turn lead into gold and NASA's space program generated a plethora of products. More recently, consider the success of your textile factory."

"I understand and agree," Paul said. "One thing certainly does seem to lead to another, and another. Knowledge tends to grow in leaps and bounds."

"Scientists all over the world are studying metamaterials and nanomaterials and we must keep abreast of these discoveries. With or without successful fabric production, important knowledge is being created. Knowledge is power, as it's always been. We have to be there to own it or we will be snuffed out of existence by those who do possess the power."

"But the quantum computer is a different story? You're recommending we proceed?" Paul leaned toward her, his eyes intense and expectant.

"Yes. What makes the difference is that with the computer, we're not trying to make quanta something they aren't. We're letting them remain subatomic particles that do strange things. We are tapping into their energy—using their strangeness, translating their tongue into a functioning language. What nanotech is trying to do with fabric is akin to trying to materialize radio waves so we can record our music on them. On the other hand, what it's trying to do with quantum computers is leave radio waves as they are and broadcast our music over them. The basis of my recommendation rests in that scenario. Let's proceed and fill the world with music."

CHAPTER 12

"Oh," Ladesque gasped. "Look at the fabric!" The sheen took her mind off her rather disturbing morning. She stopped and stared at the material winding onto the batt. Paul was touring her through the workshop, next on the agenda was a visit to the computer lab.

"Do you like it?" Paul hit a button and the machine stopped winding.

Ladesque approached the bolt and stroked the textile. "It's intriguing. I'm not sure why."

"We expect the world's top fashion designers will pay a fortune for it. Do you like the way it feels?"

She withdrew her hand and stared at the spot where her fingers had been. "It's a bit disappointing; I was expecting more. I mean, the feel is okay, cool and smooth. There's nothing repulsive about it. However, this fabric is so amazingly beautiful one expects it to feel more like heaven."

"In our apparently ill-fated mission to create a fabric that will bend light around it, we learned a lot about how light interacts with materials. We've woven together threads treated to repel light with threads that absorb light. When we hit upon the right pattern, it turned out quite nice."

"That's why it's so beautiful! Things that require interaction with the human brain are more visually appealing than solid objects. Lace, with its holes is judged beautiful because it begs the mind to fill the gaps. The fine, sparsely-placed needles of a tamarack are more appealing than the thick needles of a spruce. Newspapers and magazines know the value of leaving white space on a page to attract readers to the printed messages. Blanks encourage the human mind to fill them, and that to humans is pleasurable. This fabric is doing this, subliminally. We cannot see some threads and that draws us into the pattern. We like to merge with our surroundings, feel part of them."

Paul motioned her to step back. "Keep that thought in mind." He hit the button and the machine purred to life.

"Thoughts about beauty are always on my mind."

"I meant your thought about merging." He strode down the hall and she had to skip to keep up with him. "Keep the thought about the pleasure of merging with your surroundings in mind." He pushed open an entrance that said *Secured Area* and waved her in ahead of him.

The room they entered was dark, lit only by the blue glow from a bank of surveillance monitors covering one wall. The negative feelings that had first haunted her in Paul's office this morning, washed over her again.

She'd expected Paul to be pleased when she signed the addendum to her contract this morning in his office, agreeing to participate in her recommendation that quantum computer research be stepped up. Instead, he'd grilled her, accused her of signing before reading the entire addendum, of not understanding her commitment, of not listening to his explanations. 'You can still change your mind,' he'd offered after badgering her for a good ten minutes. 'Until this contract leaves my office, you are free to bow out of it.'

Although he may simply have been testing her commitment to the project, she got the distinct feeling he would've been happier if she hadn't signed the papers, which didn't make sense. *He knew from day one the quantum computer was my passion. Why would he now expect I would walk away from it?*

Three men swivelled their chairs to greet them. "I need a security pass for Ladesque," Paul said. "To get her into the computer lab."

"Gene will set you up," one of the three said, pointing to the guy next to him. A stocky man in his mid-forties slowly rose and beckoned Paul and Ladesque to follow. He waddled to a desk in the far corner and snapped on a desk lamp. An oval of white light spilled onto the dark mahogany.

"Who's the pass for?" Gene asked. He spun a steno chair to him from one desk over, plopped into it and fired up the computer.

"Ladesque," Paul answered. "Our new employee in the loft office above the textile floor. Put me down as her sponsor."

"La…what? How do you spell that?" A stream of employee names began rolling up his monitor.

"L-A-D-E-S-Q-U-E."

"Is that the given name or surname?"

"The only name."

"She's not listed." He quickly hit a button and the screen went blank. He stared up at Paul. The veins in his neck began visibly pulsating. "She ought not to be in this room." He was gripping the arms of his chair so hard his knuckles were white.

"Maybe I'm listed under Sally—"

"She's in there," Paul briskly interrupted. He stepped between her and Gene. "I suggest you look again."

Unnerved by the conflict, Ladesque turned her back on the men and wandered a few steps closer to the security monitors. *Is Paul's tension in here related to his anxiety in his office this morning over the addendum to my contract?*

She decided the surveillance system must be very high-tech as she'd not seen cameras anywhere on the premises yet video feed was coming in from multiple offices, dozens of hallways, every entrance and even from several locations outside the building. She squinted through the blue glare, trying to locate the picture from her office. It wasn't there.

"Ladesque!" Paul motioned her over, slapped a security card in her hand and pushed her toward the exit. He scowled over his shoulder at Gene and then hustled her out the door.

"There was a problem?" Ladesque asked.

"It's not your concern. I apologize."

"You must have very high-tech security around here. I've been looking for surveillance cameras, and haven't spotted any. However, a ton of feed is coming in."

"Yes."

"Is there a camera in my office?"

"Every office has a cam. The entire building, inside and out and up and down, is secured."

"Where is the cam in my office hidden?"

"I have no idea."

"I thought maybe there wasn't one because I didn't see any feed."

"Oh, you can bet there's one somewhere. Perhaps there's no feed because yours is one of the motion-activated cameras." They stopped in front of a set of locked double doors. He slid his and her security cards through the reader, punched in some numbers and growled 'Paul' when asked to verbally identify himself. Finally, the door swung open and he motioned Ladesque ahead of him.

"If I sit very still in my office," she said as they took up stride together, "the camera will shut down?"

"Until you move again."

"Why does anyone want video of me in my office?"

"For the protection of you and your work. We wouldn't want the highly sensitive papers and files in your office stolen or sabotaged. We also would not want you harmed, or scammed or manipulated. Visual surveillance is a great deterrent for the criminally minded."

"What about all those security guys being able to read the sensitive documents that are often strewn about my office? How secure is that?"

"Everyone who works security has top-level clearance."

"What about visitors who go in there to get their security passes? Like I just did?"

Paul said nothing, just began walking faster. Soon, she was almost running to keep up as they hurried down stairwells, along halls, through doors. She was several steps behind him and breathless when he finally slowed to navigate a steep ramp that dropped one floor down to the basement level. She caught up to him in front of the locked doors at the bottom where he was once again battling his way passed the security measures. He twice appeared to push a wrong button and when he finally removed his card key from the lock, he almost dropped it. *He's not his usual calm and cool self today...and that's making me very nervous!*

A metallic click and a blinking green light confirmed he'd completed the ritual satisfactorily. He wiped both palms on his pant legs then pushed open the door. "Go ahead," he said without glancing at her. *He hasn't looked me in the eye since he gave me my security pass.*

She stepped past him into a tunnel. Overhead, copper pipes sweated water onto the peach paint of the duct work along the ceiling edges. Paul wasted no time; as soon as the door clicked shut behind them, he was off again with Ladesque trotting to keep up.

As they scuttled past yet one more sign with colour-coded arrows pointing down an intersecting tunnel, she halted. "Paul," she said breathlessly. He stopped and looked over his shoulder. "The surveillance cameras might be high-tech but they're not being used right. If someone were to discover where a camera is hidden, they could block its view of the room with something motionless, shutting down the cam and leaving no hint something was amiss."

"What are the chances someone would discover a camera's location? You haven't been able to find the one in your office."

"One might be able to simply by calculating angles from the surveillance feed. I think the cam outside the front entrance is located—" She sprinted to catch up to him and gulped in another breath. "Probably in the dot of the 'i' in the Conroy Textiles sign. The cam in the hall leading to—"

"Remind me to instruct security to conceal the video images from visitors," Paul interrupted. He again, took off.

"Did Gene find my name in the computer?" Ladesque puffed. "Was it under Sally Jergens?"

"Don't be giving out your birth name around here. It's nobody's business." His voice was unusually harsh. "You're Ladesque and that's all anyone needs to know. And yes, you are now in the computer." He was running ahead of her, away from her. She could no longer keep up. She stopped, put her hands on her thighs and sucked in several deep breaths. The tunnel floor was bare concrete, chipped and cracked, a dull grey with spatters of paint that matched the walls and ceiling. Paul kept going.

Her excitement about the quantum computer project was fast

disappearing. Paul's nervousness was so out of character, she began to worry he was taking her somewhere other than the computer lab. However, with the doors behind her locked tight, what choice did she have but to follow him?

He was now half a block ahead. She straightened and took a few steps toward him. One of the overhead pipes groaned and her uneasiness exploded into panic. "Paul!" she screamed. Her voice echoed off the walls, the ceiling, the floor. He stopped and turned to her. "Where the hell are you taking me and what's making you so nervous?"

"Who said I'm nervous?"

The clack of her heels bit into the silence as she slowly walked toward him. He looked terrifying. Stark shadows from the overhead fluorescents mottled his face, making his forehead appear monstrously broad and concealing his chin and his nose in the shade of his brow. He was a good foot taller than her. Muscular. Strong. Just him and her in the tunnel. She wanted to run the other way, but a few feet from him, she stopped— frozen with fear.

"I'm sorry I was walking so fast," he said lightly. "My long legs make a slower pace difficult."

"Where are you taking me?"

"It's not far. Another minute or so and we'll be there."

"I thought the lab was in the same building as our offices."

"It's part of the same complex, connected by this tunnel." His tense smile was not genuine.

"What is it you haven't told me about this project?"

His gaze shifted to somewhere around her right ear. "There's lots you haven't been told. It's why we're going to the lab. You can ask whatever you want once we get there."

"Something about it is frightening you. Why?"

"High tech always involves ethical dilemmas. You noted as much in your research reports."

"Why won't you look me the eye?"

His dusky eyes zeroed in on hers. "When I look you in the eyes, you tend to interpret it as sexual." Ladesque could swear his very soul leapt the space between them and burrowed into her being. She widened her stance to keep from rushing to him and wrapping herself in him and merging. His voice was a husky whisper. Smooth. He abruptly turned and continued his brisk walk.

She stared at his back for a moment then staggered to the peach enamel-painted concrete wall, placed her back against its smooth coolness and slid to the floor. The dankness closed in around her.

She brought her knees to her chin and buried her face. *Something's so not right.* She had the distinct feeling Paul was leading her where she ought not go. From far down the corridor, a door squealed open. Metal against metal. Screech.

"Ladesque! desque…esque…" Paul's voice echoed over her, around her, past her and back.

She pulled her knees in tighter, wrapped her arms around them snugger, pushed her face between them deeper. The warmth from her underbelly carried the remnants of the rustic scent of arousal. He'd purposely looked at her that way, swallowed her whole with his eyes. Entered her, then rushed away. Why?

A flimsy three-way shadow from the staggered lights high on the ceiling, fanned across her shoes. She peeked up. He was standing over her, his head tipped to the ceiling. His eyes closed. His crotch, all zippered and hidden and tucked behind pleats was closer to her lips than his face was.

He looked down and held out his hand. "Stand up," he ordered. He grasped her fingers too tightly and pulled too quickly and too hard. And then she was standing against him. Front to front. Cheek to breast pocket. Tummy to groin. Thigh to vagina. And his arms were wrapped around her shoulders.

"You are usually so relaxed and open with me," she said.

"I'm sorry." His breath tickled at her ear.

"Are you apologizing for sins not yet committed, but that soon will be—in the computer lab?"

"No, not sins." He gently untangled his arms from her shoulders and stepped back. "You are going to be asked to play an exceptionally important and perhaps dangerous role in our quantum computer research. I'm worried for you."

Ladesque licked her lips. "How dangerous a role?"

Paul shrugged. "I don't know enough about the mechanics of the project to be able to ascertain the danger." His voice caught for just a moment and eyes flickered almost imperceptibly. "I've been advised the danger is minimal."

"Why was I not told this before?"

"It's the nature of your position, Ladesque. Some things can't be revealed until you make a commitment."

"And now it's too late for me to back down?"

"Yes. You signed your commitment letter this morning." The way he said it made it sound like a death sentence and perhaps it was. A code version of, "If I tell you, I'll have to kill you…and in moments I'll be telling you." Terrified to go forward and unable to turn back, Ladesque leaned against the wall.

"You must come with me," he said.

But she couldn't; her legs wouldn't move. If she'd listened more closely to his admonitions this morning in his office, maybe she'd have caught on. Maybe she wouldn't have signed. Maybe she'd have realized...

I can't go backwards and can't go forward, but I can go inward, as I was taught in yoga class. She once more slid to the unyielding, cold concrete. How much was she willing to risk to bring the quantum computer to life? Why had no one asked her that question before she'd been approached to sign? With her legs crossed in the lotus position, she balanced her body and closed her eyes. *In The Bible, when Adam and Eve ate the fruit from the tree of knowledge, they were evicted from paradise. What does knowledge do to man's spirit? What would the infinite knowledge generated by a quantum computer do?*

"Living is always dangerous," Paul said. "It inevitably leads to death." Ladesque inhaled and exhaled, deeply and evenly and concentrated on the rhythm of her breath. "You just might like this challenge. It might give your life the meaning you're looking for." *Breathe in the power of the universe, breathe out all tension. I need meaning, a reason to live. Is the pursuit of knowledge a worthy reason?*

"You'll be given time to adjust yourself and your life before facing the new obligations," Paul continued. "You will receive all the support you need."

One more deep breath. Mankind can survive without the internet, it's not as if my sacrifice will save the world's hungry children—or maybe with its unfathomable intelligence, the quantum computer CAN solve world hunger. Maybe it can co-ordinate an even distribution of wealth, solve the pollution crises, restock the oceans. I bet it can. "Ladesque?"

She brought her hands together at her heart. "Namaste," she whispered.

"Namaste," Paul replied. She got her feet under her and pushed herself to standing. He took her hand in his and nodded down the hall. "Shall we?"

CHAPTER 13

"It's code-named Skinner's Box," Paul said.

Her breath caught. There it was, shiny and new and farther advanced than she'd been led to believe. It looked innocuous, alone in a vault with a hundred cables, housed in a see-through red casing. The innards of the quantum computer looked nothing like those of the standard kind. She exhaled fully. "Wow." The heavy vault whooshed closed behind them, sucking out air. Ladesque's ears popped.

"It's operational," Paul said. "Has been for some time."

She slowly approached the pivotal point of power and touched the housing; it was simply plastic. There was no warmth, no breath, no pulse. It was just a machine. Her apprehension evaporated. How dangerous could it be?

"It is of course limited in its power due to having no world wide web to surf," Paul continued. "It is, however, feeding into and from the FBI's intranet system.

"What is it programmed to do?"

"It surreptitiously took over your task of protecting our intranet system from intrusions, hardware flaws and software glitches. It also covertly accesses some other intranet systems via theft of satellite and radio signals. Its top talent is deciphering codes."

Ladesque nodded. "A cyberspy." She slowly walked around the machine. What she could see of it was two feet square, sitting on a white melamine table in a pool of pink reflection. It was making no noise. She saw no monitor, mouse, or keyboard. No disks or thumb drives or air sticks. She bent and peered at the innards. It was like a little lab inside, cyclonic chambers, glass tubes. Once in a while a flash of light notified the world it was alive.

Paul drew a steno chair from against the wall and whirled it in front of the machine. "Sit," he invited.

With her eyes still on the computer, Ladesque sank into the blue cotton upholstery and rolled closer to the desk. "Do me page one of the *Getting Started Manual*. Point out the parts of machine and tell me their names."

"Later," Paul said.

"Where does it store data?"

"On the enslaved quanta captured internally."

"Enslaved?" Ladesque said. "I hardly think so. The quanta are neither enslaved nor captured."

"Domesticated?"

"That's better, but still not accurate. It really isn't us humans who have the power here. When we install solar panels, we don't say we enslaved, captured, or domesticated the sun."

"Harnessed? We are harnessing the energy and natures of quanta."

"Piggybacking. They are free and running and we're merely hitching a ride." Ladesque pulled herself closer. "No keyboard? No monitor?"

"No need," Paul said.

"Not user friendly?"

"It will be, once it gets to know you. What's the first thing you want it to do for you?"

"The first thing I want it to do? I don't know. I'm a little bit stuck in my role over at Global. It was discouraging and shaming not to be able to get the internet and wireless technology safely running again. I could do that, with Skinner's Box. If the World Wide Web was created with him and run by him, control would be his—ours. We could set the parameters, monitor for breaches, instantly shut down illicit users, block abusers, protect satellite and tower signals. Scan for competitors. That would be one use for him."

"Research?" Paul suggested. "Medicine? Forensics? Skinner's Box would make analyzing DNA a snap."

"Ah, for sure. He could even help us get quickly past the barriers to developing nano- and metamaterials. However, for the world to be safe, everything would have to be centralized. He'd have to be controlled by headquarters. Ideally, all data should be approved before being sent around the world. All uses would have to be monitored. He could be programmed so that if those checks and balances failed, for whatever reason, he'd shut down."

"He needs an overseer?" Paul suggested.

"Yes. Someone, some committee, something the world can trust. An entity who will not become corrupted by the quantum computer's power."

"Someone immortal," Paul said loudly, "so the machine would not die if those in control did."

Ladesque blinked and looked at him quizzical. "I suppose immortality would be a favourable characteristic. However, I'm not sure you'd get many applicants for the position if it was a requirement."

Paul squatted beside her chair and looked around as if to confirm no one was listening. "You are going to be digitized," he said quietly. "Immortalized."

"What?"

"Remember telling me humans find the experience of meshing with the environment pleasurable? I'm hoping your experience of melding with Skinner's Box will be more delightful than crocheted doilies and tamaracks."

"What?"

"You will be the internal overseer."

"And what happens to my non-digitized self? My mortal being? My body?"

Paul shrugged. "I don't know."

"What about the mice? The lab rats? What did they become after digitization? Where's the research on this? I must read it!"

Paul quickly stood and towered over her. "Top secret, I haven't even been allowed to see that data. It doesn't matter now, though—you've signed the consent."

"Why me?"

"The selection process was rigorous and thorough."

"I'm not the only computer geek with a genius IQ and a moral sense."

"We needed someone whose loose connections to the outer world could easily be severed."

"Loose connections?"

"We couldn't very well send a family's sole breadwinner or a mother of three off into cyberspace."

"I'm disposable?" Ladesque asked. Her heart sank to her knees. It was the last thing she'd dreamed Paul would be thinking. She'd hoped he'd noticed her new-found passion. Smelled it. Desired it. Wished to mesh and merge and mate with her. "It's because I'm a eunuch, isn't it?" Her lips were dry, her tongue thick. Her heart beat slower and slower. "Because I can't propagate and preserve my species? I can't mate and form a family and contribute to the stability of civilization? The unemployment rate is rising and jobs ought to go to those with dependents?"

"You are not disposable, Ladesque. You are vital. There are few who qualify for the position of cybernaut and even fewer who'd be willing to take it on. We need you. The world needs you. I need you."

"Need me?" Ladesque stared into his eyes. They were intense and passionate and looking past her face into her mind, imagining her a digital phantom in his super computer. *He does not see me as a woman. Not at all.* "Need me," she repeated.

That's all she was, really, wasn't it? A great mind with the incomparable ability to focus, to analyse, to predict and foresee. Her emotional nature was dulled by the absence of hormones, her passion directed to things cerebral rather than social. Yes, she was perfect for the job. Except…she felt things between her legs she ought not to be feeling.

"If you don't want the job, just say so."

"Just say so? What happens to me if I refuse?"

Paul shrugged, walked to the vault door, and swiped his security card. "You'll be a watched woman for the rest of your life. You have two weeks to get your affairs in order before the digitizing process is scheduled." He gripped the steel handle and pulled. "Go home and think about it."

"Think about what?"

"About whether you're going to honour your commitment to this project or renege and face the rather serious consequences."

"I need more information! How can I compare the danger of participating with the consequences of not when I know next to nothing about the task you're asking me to do? You said I could ask all the questions I wanted once I got here to the computer lab. What happened to that promise?"

"Ask away."

"What happened to the rats and mice and monkeys?"

"I'll see if the committee is willing to share that data with you."

"I want the raw data, Paul. Not someone's interpretation of the results, not the white-washed version."

He motioned her out of the vault. "No more talking about it until we get back to my office. The concrete tunnels interfere with electronics to the point our privacy is not ensured."

She heard him mumble something to himself as she edged past him. It sounded like he said, *"Please tell me I haven't made the wrong decision."*

Neither of them said anything for a long time once they got back to his office. Paul took up his favourite pose in front of his window, looking out over the city, with his hands shoved deep into his pant pockets. Ladesque sat in her usual chair across from his desk, counting floor tiles and memorizing their pattern.

"I don't think the committee will hand over the info you've requested," Paul finally said. "Especially if it finds out you're double-thinking your commitment to the project. It's highly sensitive research that should not be in the hands of anyone not directly involved in bringing Skinner's Box on stream."

"I overheard you mumbling you hoped you hadn't made a wrong decision. What's to keep *me* from making the wrong decision when such important information is being kept hidden from me?"

"Ladesque," he turned to her and sighed. "When I speak to you about this project, I am speaking on behalf of the committee. It's my job to support and communicate the committee's decisions even if they don't all reflect my personal ones. A tremendous amount of work went into analysing the position you're being offered and in choosing you as the best-qualified person. You could say we looked the world over and decided there was none better for the job than one of our own. If you decline to proceed, many will be disappointed. Much labour and many dollars will have been wasted. The Skinner's Box project will be delayed indefinitely and, delaying this project, as I'm sure you realize, endangers the world. Who knows how close to fruition other researchers in other nations are? You and I both know the first one out of the gate with this computer will be the one who will hold the power. Others may follow, but if Skinner's Box is first, it will make sure all others do indeed follow and not lead. This project is imperative and time-sensitive and your refusal to commit is serious. Ladesque, you SAW Skinner's Box. You touched it. You've been apprised of the next step in the project. Now is not a safe time for you to back away from it."

"Could they force me to do it? Do they have the technology to incapacitate me in order to digitize my mind against my will and feed it into Skinner's Box? Is my free will in this matter a mere illusion and this two weeks reprieve, simply the time I'm being allowed to write a will and dispose of my assets?"

"You can do whatever you want these next two weeks—take a vacation if you desire, visit your home town." Paul slumped into his chair and picked up a pen. "I can't tell you what will happen if you renege on your commitment. Although because of secrecy, the committee doesn't have the option of using the courts to force you to comply with your signed contract, perhaps it has other means of enforcement at its disposal, technical or otherwise."

"What's the decision that *you* are second guessing?"

"Your selection!" Paul shouted. He threw his pen down so hard it rolled from his desk and clattered to the floor. "I pushed you onto the committee! I did all I could to ensure you were considered the top candidate."

"Why? Because I'm a eunuch? Dispensable?"

"No! Because I've seen your work, Ladesque. When I was with Global, I saw your determination to get the internet up and running again. I saw your dedication, the hours you spent both salvaging the data from the old internet and programming the new. Your anonymous, uncompromised, selfless labour to get the world back online—safely. With no thought of personal reward or recognition. With no bending to government, commercial, public, or peer pressure. I wanted to give all that to the committee. But more than that, Ladesque. I wanted to give to you the opportunity to achieve the goal you've worked so many years to attain.

It seemed a perfect match, for both parties. When you told me of your passionate interest in the quantum computer..." He leaned back in his chair and all intensity dropped from his face. "So, *you* tell me, did I make the wrong decision?"

Ladesque stretched her leg and, using her shoe pulled his fallen pen toward her. She picked it up and rose. "All things considered, including the danger..." She threw his pen to his desk. It bobbled and bounced, hit him in the chest and disappeared somewhere down toward his lap. "I don't see how you can even begin to think that decision was yours to make!"

CHAPTER 14

Ladesque barely had her coat off before her door buzzer sounded. She froze; terrified Paul had changed his mind about her two-week reprieve and sent someone for her. It was Roach's voice, however, that came over the intercom. "Ladesque, open up. I know you're home. I saw you walk in."

Relief put a smile on her face as she flung open the door. Roach stood on the step with a silly grin, his head cocked, a six pack of *CANADIAN* brand beer under his arm. "Need some cheering?" he asked.

"How the hell did you know?" She motioned him in. Roach definitely lacked the beautiful symmetry of Paul. He was too short for his weight and one shoulder drooped lower than the other. His smile was crooked and there was a space where his right eye tooth ought to be. Plus, he smelled like day-old sweat.

"A hunch," he said. "Brought you some of your home-country brew. I was told this is the best beer made in the Great White North." Canadian beer wasn't easy to find and it cost twice as much as domestic beer. He'd gone out of his way for her.

"It'll do," she said. Her arms and her belly tingled at the thought she had a friend. "Come in. Have a seat."

Roach set the beer on the coffee table, snapped open a can for each of them, and then sprawled on her sofa. He took a quick swallow and flicked his eyes over her face and chest as if he judged her attractive. She presumed if he had a bit more self-confidence, his gaze would've been more steady, more intimate. She wondered if he considered her his friend or if his visit was more about going out with his buddies tomorrow and bragging about drinking beer the night before with a hot FBI chick.

"So…" He kicked off his shoes and placed his feet on the coffee table. "What's the matter?"

"I didn't say anything is the matter."

"I was told you needed cheering. Casper's job isn't turning out all that well?"

"Who told you I need cheering?"

"I don't reveal my sources."

Ladesque sighed and tugged at the decorative afghan folded over the back of the sofa. She was chilled, perhaps because of the stress of the day or maybe because she was holding a cold beer. She switched her beer to the other hand and smoothed the afghan over her lap. "I can't reveal anything, either, Roach. I don't work for Global any more. Our secrets are no longer the same." The can was weeping condensation. Now both hands were wet. She wiped one, then the other on her shirt.

"I know," he said softly. He swung his feet to the floor and leaned toward her. "There has to be something, though, that we can talk about?"

She wished he'd get up and come over and give her a hug, take the cold beer from her hand and snuggle up beside her under the afghan. He stood, raised and lowered his arms as if a fledgling preparing for flight, and walked away from her to the window.

His silhouette against the setting November sun was lopsided and plump around the middle. The structure of his butt was hidden behind baggy cotton pants which were the colour of un-dyed canvass. She wanted to walk to him, press against his warmth, wrap her arms around his soft belly, lean her head on his shoulder. She wanted...

"Thanks for the beer," she said. "It's special that you thought to bring me some."

"Special beer for a special lady," he said, keeping his back to her.

"How is your God program coming?"

He shrugged and then bowed his head to check his toes.

"Are you here because I'm a safe date?" Ladesque asked.

He half turned to her. "What do you mean?"

"Like, because I'm a eunuch I won't be putting you in any awkward situations. You won't have to decide whether or not to kiss me or whether or not I want to 'do it' with you...and stuff."

He turned to her. "I'm here as a friend, Ladesque." He jammed his hands in his pockets and rested his butt against the window ledge.

"I'm a safe friend? A safe 'female' friend?"

"If I didn't think you were safe, you wouldn't be my friend."

"I'm not talking about 'safe' like you won't end up in a morgue. I mean 'safe' like your ego won't get crushed and your heart broken." He scrunched his face as if he didn't understand. "If I weren't a eunuch," she continued, "would you be sitting over here, beside me with your arm around my shoulders?"

"Perhaps...if you were to let me...in such circumstances."

She patted the space beside her on the sofa. "Come then," she said. "Sit. I need someone to hold me."

It was as delicious as she'd imagined. As soon as she'd covered them both with the afghan, he wrapped her in his arms. She rested her head on his chest and closed her eyes. Behind the soft wool of his vest, his heart pumped strong and steady. He began to caress her shoulder.

Beneath his touch, her icy tension melted into tears. "That feels good," she sobbed.

"Sssshh," he soothed. "It's okay. It's going to be okay."

"I was told today I was dispensable and disposable with ties that could easily be severed. I believed it was true. Is it, Roach? Would you miss me if I weren't here?"

"The world would miss you, Ladesque. Who told you such an evil thing?"

"Someone who knows."

"Knows what?"

"Just...knows."

He placed his hands on her shoulders and pushed her gently away. His blue eyes were on hers, misty and hazy. "Can I kiss you?" he asked.

She nodded and closed her eyes. His lips were delicious. Warm and engorged. Soft. Teasingly gentle for such a long time. She held her breath. Waiting. Waiting for more, for harder. For deeper. But he pulled away and wiped a curl from her cheek.

She slowly opened her eyes. Nestled behind the blue of his, was hesitancy. Kindness. Happiness. Friendship, perhaps. "Thank you," she whispered.

CHAPTER 15

Ladesque pulled the pillow over her eyes to block out the rising sun. She did not want to get up. She could contentedly stay curled forever beneath the flannel sheets and down duvet, by herself, in a dream world made cosier by her first romantic kiss.

However, those hot lips of hers were now dry from slumber and her tongue, thick. She needed a drink of water and two mugs of coffee. She thought of a slice of toast with cream cheese as she reluctantly put her feet on the floor. Out her window, far beyond the house across the street, toward the west, across the flat prairie, the city limits brushed up against the Rockies.

She thought maybe she'd visit the mountains today to seek their comfort and wisdom. Perhaps she was crazy, but when she touched their granite, she heard their stories.

Although their birth had been violent, the years since had honed their peaks and softened their shoulders. Today, they towered above their people, massive and silent and unmoving. They controlled the rivers and the rainfall, the wind and weather for an entire continent. Basking in their shadows and breathing their air was intimidating. However, the closer one moved toward their cliffs, the closer one came to sharing their energy. "Lean your back against their rocks," someone once said, "and their wisdom is yours."

Ladesque wandered into the kitchen and set the coffee. Last night had ended so sweetly. After the kiss, Roach had finished his beer, gave her the remaining *CANADIAN* for 'next time' and left. She'd followed him to the door, wishing he'd stay but unsure how to tell him. He'd skipped down her front steps, stuck his hands in his pockets, and began whistling. 'Roach!' she'd called when he reached the sidewalk. He quit whistling and turned to her. 'You're out of the contest.'

'How so?'

'You helped an FBI agent. I asked for a hug and you gave me one.'

His lopsided grin looked so adorable. 'Yeah, you're right.'

She grabbed her mug of coffee and slid into a kitchen chair. Roach had been so in tune with her and she, him. It had been more about hearts and emotions, friendship and fears than about the stuff between her legs. Roach cared about her, all of her. It had been much richer an experience than the time she'd spent with Paul. It had not been just about body parts or her genius. He cared about her in a magnanimous way. Yet it had been more than a sexless friendship. There had been the kiss.

Her weather radio beeped and the robotic voice enunciated a heavy snowfall warning for later that day. The first winter storm of the year was going to be a big one. Ladesque sighed. That meant no trip to the mountains for her. She'd be stuck in her house, alone with her unanswered questions and unfathomable choices.

It was later, after she was showered and dressed and had taken to staring at the blue snow clouds rolling in, that thoughts of her mother resurfaced. If there was anything she ought to do during her two-week reprieve, it was uncover the mysteries surrounding her mother. She had several cardboard boxes stored in the basement, stuff she'd hauled home after her father's death. Some of the boxes contained things that she'd packed herself. However, a few of them were ones she'd found hidden behind a panel at the back of her mother's closet.

At the time, she'd peaked in the boxes. One was filled with what looked like her mother's work-related papers and notes. Another box had craft supplies. One had newspaper clippings. She'd been grieving, alone, and not interested in reading further.

She was interested now, though. She'd not been able to find her mother in the tenth floor archived copies of cyberspace. Perhaps the information she wanted was in one of the boxes. She wasn't sure what it was she hoped to find, perhaps some clue as to what Paul and Marielle thought her mother knew about her asexuality. Maybe some information that would explain the swift, intense changes taking over her anatomy. Or proof her mother had loved her. That to at least someone in the world, she'd been as wonderful as anybody else, as needed, as useful, and as human—perfectly fine just the way she was.

She clicked on the staircase light and trudged to the basement, which was dark, unfinished and had tiny windows that never let in much sun. It was home to the furnace and hot water tank and other sources of mechanical noises that sometimes scared her at night. The concrete floor and walls were dry and chalky.

She pulled the sturdiest of the boxes from under the stairs to sit on and then tugged out another and ripped it open. It was filled with her mother's research papers. They were bound together in transparent plastic covers with expandable plastic spines. Each portfolio bore the stamp of the McGill University Human Sexuality Research Centre in Montreal.

The first one she flipped open was a research grant application that bore the giant red 'DENIED' stamp across the cover page. The proposal was for a study of asexuality in females. Although her mother obviously would've been interested in the subject, given her daughter was among those so afflicted, the proposal was written when Ladesque was only ten—three years before she'd been diagnosed. Perhaps suspicions about an emerging generation of asexual females existed long before it happened. Perhaps researchers were hoping to find a way to prevent the inevitable. If she ever got back into that tenth floor vault she wanted to see how much was known about female asexuality prior to her diagnosis.

A checklist tucked behind the cover listed the reasons why a grant application may be rejected. Topping the list of reasons was *'Proposal research is too similar to other projects'*, followed by *'Required data missing.'* However, none of the reasons were ticked. She flipped the sheet over but all that was on the back was some doodling across the top.

Several portfolios dealt with research on homosexual relationships and one addressed fetishes—which reminded her of the 2010 Colonel Williams news story and his obsession with silky ladies' underwear.

Buried beneath the slick presentation folders was a black, hard-covered diary. It was locked with a clasp Ladesque knew she could easily cut open if she had some wire snippers. However, she wondered if she ought to open it. Her mother had obviously considered whatever she'd written to be private. She flipped the diary over and pried at the cover. She could see gilt-edged pages but the writing remained out of sight.

She strained at the lock with her fingers and even tried her teeth. Legally, dead people had no rights to privacy but morally…She set the book aside and ripped open another box. A pattern book for crocheted doilies was on top and beneath it, a set of crochet hooks. She dug deeper and found a glue gun, some white ribbon, and a pair of needle-nosed pliers. Ladesque fingered the pliers, wondering if they were strong enough to break the diary lock.

She rummaged through the tangled balls of wool and cotton, and the buttons and bows. Were there other tools she could use? *Yes!* A pair of heavy-duty craft scissors and a razor knife. She now ought to be able to unlock her mother's secrets.

With the knife, she dug into the leather binding around the lock and deep into the cardboard cover below. She grasped the lock with the pliers and tugged. The still-locked clasp broke free and dangled from its back cover counterpart. She opened the diary.

Her mother's name and birthday, beautifully scripted in aqua ink adorned the first page. Mesmerized, she rose and slowly walked to the stairs. She briefly looked down to set her foot firmly on the bottom step. That was the last time her eyes left the diary until the clock struck 9:00 p.m.

The softness of the sofa that had initially cradled her comfortably was now, six hours later, playing havoc with her spine. She slowly set her feet on the floor and dropped the diary onto the coffee table.

The entries started with Ladesque's birth and ended just weeks before her mother's death—at least that's what Ladesque figured. Halfway through the book, shortly after the note about taking her adolescent daughter for hormone testing, the script changed from English to strange nicks, squiggles, lines, and dots.

Ladesque had carefully scanned each page, looking for patterns, looking for links, deciphering the little she could. She hadn't been very successful. A quantum computer would've had the translation done in less than a second. She yawned. Although she was tired beyond tired, she knew the strange symbols were going to race around her head all night, keeping her from restful slumber.

She walked to the kitchen, poured a glass of milk, and grabbed an apple. Perhaps by morning, her subconscious mind would have the code deciphered.

Most of the diary entries she could read were focussed on her—her successes and failures, activities and plans. Her first smile, her first steps, her first day of school. It was obvious her mother had adored her—at least when she'd been a child. The fact the script became encoded after the hormonal testing bothered Ladesque. Had her mother's feelings towards her changed after that? Had she felt angry? Embarrassed? Guilty? Hurt?

When Ladesque had hit her teens, she hadn't noticed any change in the way her mother treated her. On the other hand, she also hadn't noticed how much her mother had adored her in the first place.

She'd never been very close to her father—a distant, hard-working man who travelled lots and talked little. She remembered as a small child her mother calling him old-fashioned and chiding him about his flip phone and lack of computer skills. After the collapse of cyberspace, he'd tell people he was one of the few smart enough to see it coming.

He'd always treated Ladesque gently and carried her picture in his wallet. But she didn't know his true thoughts about her. Had guilt been on his conscience? Blame? Was he happy his daughter was safe from the vulgarities of sexuality or did he view her as less than feminine? A useless, empty vessel that would never pass on his genes? Did he care about her in any way, good or bad?

She stumbled to her room, stripped, and crawled between the cool sheets. She clapped her hands. "Lights off!" she ordered. As the room darkened, she pulled the blankets over her bare shoulders, closed her eyes to dancing dots and dashes, and was instantly asleep.

CHAPTER 16

Ladesque awoke bleary eyed in the morning, confused by the images circling in her brain. The dream spirits had left her without words, just nameless emotions and a sense of doom. It seemed the coded markings in her mother's diary were related somehow to research, something about an experiment gone dreadfully wrong. Something.

She kicked off the covers and hit the remote control by the pillow. The blinds slowly lifted. Wave after white wave of snow, sculpted overnight by the wind, fluted the street and the prairie beyond. The distant mountains were bathed in bright sunlight—crystalline peaks against a cerulean sky.

The snow would likely be gone by tomorrow; a Colorado winter was silent snow sweeping in from the Rockies one day then disappearing beneath a Chinook the next.

Ladesque set her feet on the floor. What was it she wanted to do? Visit the Rockies? Get into the tenth floor vault? Go through some more of her mother's stuff? Perhaps a note that explained the coded entries in the diary was buried in one of the boxes. Perhaps she'd find a clue about the name her mother went by on the social networks. She must have had a blog, a Facebook page, a Twitter account. Something, anything that might explain why her eunuch daughter suddenly craved the company of men. Something about her mother's own connection to the FBI. Something....

Ladesque threw on her robe, padded barefoot through to the kitchen and set the coffee. As it brewed, she picked up the diary and, using the images left from sleep, tried to decipher the entries. The cadence and rhythm of the strokes, the repetitions and punctuation, suggested to Ladesque the script was based on English, but was it phonetic—did the characters represent sounds? Or words? Perhaps, entire ideas? If she deciphered a few of the marks, would the code unravel easily?

Here and there, an English word appeared on the page. A 'Sally' here and a 'Montreal' there—tantalizing clues that proved to be of little help.

She closed the diary and poured a coffee. Where would she find the help she needed? In the vault? In Montreal? In a box in her basement? The phone rang and she answered.

"Hey," Roach's slow voice offered. "Whatcha up to?"

"Hello," she reluctantly answered. What Roach felt towards her—a supposedly sexless woman—was another puzzle, one she didn't want to work on at this moment.

"You're doing nothing?"

"I'm thinking!" The crisp edge to her voice surprised her. She'd not meant to sound angry. She cleared her throat. "Roach, I've got something to ask. Could I...would it be alright if I came to the office and looked up something on those archived internet files. It has nothing to do with the FBI—"

"Ladesque, we have different secrets, now. You can't just—"

"For me, Roach. A personal request. I was told I had two weeks to get my personal life in order before...never mind. I need to do this. I need to find some information on my mother. She's dead and I'm grieving her right now and...whatever. Please?"

"I'll have to get permission. Do you want....What are you doing tonight?"

"Nothing planned."

"We could do something together. Maybe?"

"Maybe. Find out for me right now, okay?"

"I'll take you to dinner—"

"Just find out, Roach. Then we'll talk." Ladesque hung up and immediately felt guilty. This would never have happened a couple of months ago. She was using Roach's attraction to her, to get what she wanted. She was rewarding him with promises of her company. She was....

Lordy. She sank into her chair and stared at the snow—brilliant and blinding beneath the noon sun.

How did the world survive when human behaviour was so centred on sex? Not just consensual behaviour in the bedroom, but manipulative behaviour, such as hers and Roach's, in the boardrooms of the nation. She tied her robe tighter, took a big slurp of hot coffee, and curled her feet under her butt. Just looking at the snow made her cold. She ought to go steam in the shower for a bit and get dressed.

The phone rang again and Roach began before she'd said hello. "The answer's no, Ladesque. Sorry. I tried—"

"How about you sneak me in?"

"Yeah, right! You're not the one who'd get fired."

"I'm sorry." Ladesque sighed. "Really, Roach. I'm sorry I asked you to do that."

"Talon says the only way he'll let you in is if he gets a formal request from your FBI bosses. Then, he'll consider it."

"Then I'll get him his damned formal request!" Ladesque set her cup down noisily and pushed back her chair.

"About dinner tonight—" Roach started before she clicked off the phone and headed to the shower.

~ * ~

She caught Paul standing at his office window staring out at the winter wonderland. He looked ultra symmetric against the white banks and blue shadows. She cleared her throat and he turned.

His eyes were bright today, almost dancing. And his dimple was showing. "Ladesque! Great to see you. Have you—"

"I need to get in the tenth floor vault to research the archived copies of the internet," she interrupted.

He raised his eyebrows. An amused grin replaced his pleased smile. "Why?"

She'd like to feel those smiling lips just below her right earlobe. The heat of his breath catching at the fine hairs that curled about her neck....

She shivered. "I need to research what was known about quantum computers and digitization prior to the economic and internet collapse to ascertain the significance of the project in which I'm being required to participate. By studying the history of this technology, I'll be able to more accurately forecast its future and thus help with my decision—"

"Bullshit," Paul said. He waved her to sit and then dropped into the chair behind his desk. "At what point in time do you intend on being honest with me?" He smelled good. Not scented or perfumed. Just a natural, rustic, man-smell.

"Honest with you?"

"It has to be soon, Ladesque. Very soon."

"Or there will be serious repercussions?"

"Honesty is imperative when people are working together on an ultra-sensitive project—"

"I haven't yet agreed to work on the project."

"I see. We're still at that point, are we?"

"Before I advance past that point, I need to research my mom. I need to understand my history so I can make good decisions about my future."

"Ah." Paul clasped his hands behind his head and leaned back in his chair. His chest muscles strained at his top shirt buttons.

"I apologize for lying about my reasons. However, I'm desperate to get into those files and had to come up with a reason that would net me the formal FBI request Talon says I need."

"Why are you desperate to research your mother?"

"Because people, including you, keep hinting my mother had something to tell me. Since she's dead and nobody seems forthcoming with more information...What do you know about my mother?"

"Probably less than you do."

"But more than you know about, say, Roach's mom?"

"I know your mom through her research papers." Paul thumped his chair forward, slid a file toward him, and reached for a pen.

"What kind of research papers of hers were you reading? Was she was involved in metamaterial research? Nanotech?"

"No."

"Computers?"

"No. Human sexuality and you can't tell me you didn't know that."

"I just found that out by going through her papers. How did you find out?"

"I have my ways."

"Why would Mom's human sexuality research interest you? It's not in your line of work. It's not related to technology at all."

"All science is interrelated—a fact with which we soon have to come to grips. When an archaeologist doesn't understand the true nature of time, you can imagine how inaccurate and skewed his view of history becomes."

"But how does human sexuality relate to what you're doing?"

"To understand the human heart and mind is to understand the quantum computer."

"Great. Then, I assume I'll get your formal request for vault access?"

"Not right now," Paul said.

"But—"

"I said, not now."

Ladesque rose and, placing her hands on his desk, narrowed her eyes and leaned into him. "Are you scared I'll find something that will keep me out of your computer?"

"I didn't say that."

"What reason then, Paul, do you have to deny me access? Why are you trying to shield me from information about my mother?"

"Perhaps it's not about your mother. Perhaps it's about other things in the archived files. Perhaps—"

Ladesque pounded her fist on the desk. "Bullshit."

Paul stood and came around the desk. She straightened and turned to meet him. She felt his warmth as he neared. He stopped inches from her. "When the time is right, I'll get you your access." He walked to the door and opened it. "I suggest you don't show up here again until you have a decision for me."

"Fine." Ladesque whisked passed him. "Fine."

CHAPTER 17

Ladesque had called the airport and booked the earliest flight out to Montreal and the red-eye back home. With the assistance of time zones, she ought to have enough hours to do what she needed to do. Paul had said she could visit her home town, so she ought to be okay leaving the country but she was slightly afraid if she plotted an overnighter across the border she might end up shackled in some Customs backroom on one side of the border or the other. All those concerns aside, she had too much to do back here in Colorado to take a vacation—too many life and death decisions to make, plus a plot to hatch to get into the tenth floor vault.

Four a.m. came early. She pinched back her front curtain. The same grey sedan that had been there all week was still there, spotlighted by the streetlight. A puff of exhaust divulged the fact someone was inside it—trying to keep warm and likely trying to stay alert.

She called a taxi, checked her wallet for money and credit cards, and rummaged through the contents in her safe to get her passport. Someday she'd have to sort through the stack of papers that took up most of the space. Many of them related to her father's financial affairs and the probating of his will. She likely could throw most of them away now. Outside the sun was struggling to break through the clouds and the grey sedan was still at the curb across the street. She dragged her winter coat from the closet and tossed it over the railing.

She needed something to do on the plane during the four hour flight. She ran down the basement and searched through her mother's boxes. She might as well spend the time getting to know her mother; after all, that was the purpose of her mission. She grabbed a stack of worn paperbacks just as the door bell rang. Reading the same books as one's mother read was about as close a connection as a daughter could make; stories were known to create bonds between their readers. She'd feel as her mother felt when the words unravelled, relaying emotions, teaching lessons, exploring human nature. It was just too bad she'd never get to discuss the novels with her mom.

She dug out five books, fled up the stairs and greeted the taxi driver. "No luggage," she said, grabbing her coat and purse. She slipped into her boots, slung her purse over her shoulder and, rushed out the door. The sedan across the street purred to life. It was obviously not meant to be a secret that she was being watched. *I hope they let me leave the U.S. Since I'm Canadian, they have to let me travel to my own country, don't they?*

As the taxi merged into the stream of traffic filling the freeway to the Denver airport, Ladesque glanced back. The sedan was definitely on their tail. She looked anxiously at her watch, the meter, the horizon—where she willed the famous white peaks of the Denver terminal to appear. Behind her, the sedan still followed.

Forty-five minutes later, her taxi pulled to the curb at the terminal. Ladesque pressed the fare into the driver's hand and without glancing back, slipped from the cab and raced through the big glass doors. She immediately stepped to the side and pressed her back to the wall. For five minutes she kept her eyes on all who came through the entrance. At last, convinced no one was following her, she exhaled a sigh of relief and took off to find the ticket counter.

Despite her fears, she cleared security easily. However, she didn't relax until she felt the familiar drop in her tummy as the plane's wheels lifted from the tarmac. She settled back in her window seat, closed her eyes and slowed her breathing. She was going to Montreal and no one could stop her now.

Once the plane quit banking and slowed its ascent, she opened her eyes. Below her, the land had disappeared beneath a rolling cloudscape and around her people shuffled their feet and unlocked the snack trays.

She retrieved her books from under the seat, knowing since she was near the rear of the plane it would be forever before the flight attendants reached her with their trolley of free juice and dry cookies. Although she'd lived with her mother for eighteen years, she didn't feel she knew her well. She'd only seen her mother through the eyes of child.

The cover of the first paperback was ripped and wrinkled and sported an indistinct countryside. On the back, a subdued review touted it as 'one of Canada's finest in literary fiction'. *'Historical romance,'* the back cover copy read. *'A prairie love affair on hold until the Great War ended.'* She flipped past the credits to page one. The low-quality pages were yellowed and the ink was sinking into the soft grain, distorting the font.

Not one for either romance or war stories, she pulled out the second book. It was a pinkish-orange hardcover, rough and tough like a text book—built to last. *New Basic Course in Pitman Shorthand* was the title and that was all that was on the cover. The book fell open somewhere toward the middle. Ladesque gasped.

The page was filled with the same squiggles and dots that were in her mother's diary. She turned back to the beginning pages. They were full of English words and phrases, interspersed with squiggles. *'I', 'may', 'may be', 'I maybe'.*

Spread across the inside cover and the first page was a table entitled, *'Short Forms'.* The table was nine columns wide and fifteen rows deep with a character in each square. In tiny script in the right corner above the graph, was her grandmother's name, Alison Crate, inscribed in a blue ink that was turning green with time.

Ladesque recalled she was named after both her mother and her grandmother. Alison, Alice, and Sally, her mom had told her, were variations of the same name.

She flipped back and forth from the short form chart to the explanatory pages. The marks could apparently represent sounds, letters, words, or phrases.

'To The Student,' she read in the forward. *'About Pitman Shorthand. From the day of its conception in 1837, Pitman Shorthand has been used by office workers and court reporters...to record a dozen languages....'*

On the copyright page, it was noted the book had been printed and bound in Toronto in 1964. She imagined Pitman Shorthand had been a secretary's best friend before recording devises were invented and before computer keyboards sat on bosses' desks.

'Be proud of the system you are about to study, confident in the knowledge that it is capable of recording the words of even the fastest speakers...'

For her mother it had come in handy another way—as a code no one of her generation would be able to decipher.

Ladesque skimmed through the shorthand lessons which started out with the symbols for 'to, 'the', of'. The book referred to the marks as 'outlines.' The lessons became progressively more difficult as common words were connected to form common phrases. Overall, though, it was a phonetic code, the marks representing sounds, consonants, vowels, blended sounds.

The marks themselves were important, but equally so were their placements—above the line, below the line or on the line—whether they were light or dark (shaded), and if they were positioned before or after, above or below, other symbols.

Three hours later, when she'd finished reading all the lessons, she drew a pen from her purse and carefully wrote her name in Pitman Shorthand on the back cover. *'Sally'.* The group of symbols was very familiar. They'd appeared often in her mom's diary.

She squeezed her eyes shut. Desperate to know what secrets her mother had written, she tried to call to mind the symbols in the diary but remembered too few of them. Frustrated, she squeezed her eyes tighter. Suddenly, perhaps because she'd stared at them often, the exact marks on the paper rejecting her mom's research proposal appeared. She slowly translated them in her mind. '*Approval rescinded due to lawsuit.*'

Who had been suing who, and why?

CHAPTER 18

The Montreal Arts Faculty looked dull, drab and old with its grey walls, patina roof, gothic columns, and constrained windows. Ladesque took a deep breath and marched toward it. *Age and wisdom and cold stone steps are so intimidating.*

Once inside, however, it was not all that foreboding. The art students had done an amazing job of enlivening the interior. She followed the arrows through hallways and foyers and timidly knocked on the human sexuality research lab door.

She pushed against the heavy oak and peeped in. It was not a lab with Bunsen burners and jars of liquids and powders, but rather a busy office. Just inside, a woman behind the front desk rose. "May I help you?" she asked. She was about Ladesque's age, with black silky waves of hair sweeping over her shoulders and down her back. Her tresses moved in the light, as if liquid.

Ladesque stepped in. Behind her, the door slammed shut with a squeal and clang. Ladesque jumped. "I'm so sorry. I—"

The woman waved off her apology. "Don't worry. It happens all the time. We submitted a request to maintenance to fix the hinge, but they haven't yet arrived. Perhaps it's not in the budget. May I help you?"

Ladesque stepped closer, attracted to her warmth. She smelled faintly of sea spray. Her eyes were oval and dark. Symmetric. Beautiful. Ladesque held out her hand. "I'm Sally Jergen's."

"Rachelle," the woman greeted in turn. Her handshake was firm and warm.

"My mother worked here fifteen or so years ago as a researcher," Ladesque said. "She died a while back."

"I'm very sorry to hear that."

"I miss her. I'm disappointed I didn't get the chance to establish an adult relationship with her. I want to get to know her better—as a woman, not just a mom. I'm on a quest to discover all I can about her."

"I see."

"I'm interested in learning about the research projects she worked on."

Rachelle returned to her seat and pulled her keyboard to her. "I'll see if I can find her in our records. Tell me, Sally, what was your mother's name?"

"Alice Jergens."

"Ah, yes, here she is. A busy lady, it appears. She's listed as researcher, author, and co-author on several projects. I'll print this list for you and show you to the library, where you can find the reports."

Rachelle made Ladesque comfortable at a large desk in the center of the library, explained the setup and handed her the printout. "I'll be at my desk if you need help," she whispered, turning to leave. Ladesque watched her retreat, amazed the sound of her footsteps was totally absorbed by the thick navy carpet. The library's acoustics were unnerving, so quiet Ladesque felt her very breath was being absorbed by the walls. *I'm going to fricken suffocate in here!*

She forced herself to inhale deeply and then glanced around the room. It was about twenty feet by twenty feet. A small table with a half-dozen chairs nestled against the far wall below the windows and a couple of carrels filled the corner to her right. However, as far as Ladesque could see, nobody else was in the room.

She grabbed Rachelle's list and began to work her way through the projects. She was impressed at how well organized and cross-referenced the extensive library records were. It was going to make her task much quicker and easier than she'd anticipated.

The first report she located was her mother's 2010 fetish research project. She was interested to discover fetishism is one of the most treatable of sexual deviancies. If Colonel Williams had sought help with his obsessions, his victims could very well have avoided their dates with trauma and death.

Ladesque's familiarity with the terminology increased as she made her way down the list of her mother's credits. Soon it became clear none of the research mentioned female asexuality. She re-shelved the papers and headed back to Rachelle's desk.

"Are all the research records in this library?" Ladesque asked.

"Yes. Originals never leave here, only copies can be signed out."

"I noticed there are research proposals as well as reports are on the shelves. Are all proposals kept?"

"Oh, yes. Proposals take a lot of work and time. Sometimes rejected proposals get a second life with a bit of rewording or a change in circumstances."

"I found a copy of a proposal in my mother's papers that I can't locate in your library. It was on female asexuality."

"Perhaps it's one she ended up not submitting. Otherwise, we would have a record of it."

"But it had a denied stamp on it with the McGill logo."

"There's the possibility she worked here but was being paid by someone besides the university—in which case the record-keeping would be different. Back then, private companies sometimes contracted our researchers and facilities. That practice, once a major fundraiser for the research department, no longer exists. Shortly after the Great Crash, the ethics board decided that because the results of corporately-sponsored research were often viewed as biased and tainted, we no longer wanted our department to be associated with it."

"How would I find out if my Mom was hired by a corporation to do research?"

"Such research and the associated results and reports were deemed to belong to the company that paid for them. Many corporations left us a library copy of the research as a courtesy. However, if the research results were unfavourable, they sometimes pulled all records of the project from our system."

"What would be considered an 'unfavourable' result?"

"An example would be if a drug company asked for research on a new product and our experiments proved it to be ineffective, harmful or not economically feasible. Positive results were sometimes hidden, too, in order to keep them secret from the competition."

"Would the administration have any information on such secret projects?"

"You might be able to track down who funded a project by looking at financial records. Since research proposals are labour intensive and costly to produce, whoever paid for them likely kept copies, as well. I'm not sure how you'd track that, though, if there's no mention of a corporation on the copy you have."

"I didn't notice any corporate name."

"You might be able to find if your mother had a link to a corporation from the records in Administration. Our scientists usually don't take on projects outside the university but if they are particularly interested in a subject, they may move on if they find funding elsewhere. In the research field, contacts are vital so Administration keeps somewhat of a Who's Who list of past employees."

"Thank you for all your help."

"Did your mother attend McGill as a student?"

"I'm not sure. Why?"

"If she did, you could try the Alumni Office in the Students Union Building. It's notorious for keeping track of graduates. They might have a record of corporate links to your mother. However, I suggest you first try Administration's Who's Who list. It's more likely to have the kind of information you're looking for."

~ * ~

"We're not here to track genealogy," the woman at the Administration reception desk said when Ladesque introduced herself and outlined her quest.

"I'm not tracking genealogy, I'm tracking research. I already know my lineage."

The woman waved to a computer in the far corner. "That kind of public information is stored in our intranet main frame. You don't need a password, just use the search feature to find the biography on your mom, if there is one."

It startled Ladesque when her search yielded a full-screen picture of her mother, smiling a professional, distant smile. Her dark curls were brushing the translucent white collar of her lab coat. She looked efficient and proficient and had not attended McGill as a student but was rather a graduate of Harvard, with a PhD in Human Sciences. *She had her doctorate! I didn't know that.* She'd worked at several university labs before coming to McGill.

Although her services with McGill's Human Sexuality Research Centre were noted, no mention was made of any research or employment following her stint with McGill and no mention of any female asexuality project. Her mother's last listed project was the 2010 one on fetishes, then she abruptly disappeared from the administration's computer.

Perhaps Harvard had kept track of her longer. *Or, since I'm here, maybe I should try to uncover the money trail.*

Ladesque slowly rose and, weary and discouraged, once more approached the Administration receptionist. The woman kept her eyes on her monitor, her face skewed as if she were listening intently to the telephone cradled on her shoulder, her fingers poised above her keyboard. "Excuse me," Ladesque began, "can you—"

"One moment," the receptionist tersely interrupted.

Ladesque looked at her watch. She had little time before she had to catch her flight. She thumped her fingers impatiently on the counter. The woman finally looked up. "Where would I find the university's financial reports and records of lawsuits launched by or against McGill?"

"That wouldn't be here," the clerk whispered. She looked again to her monitor and giggled into the handset. "You're such a devil. How about we meet at Kyrow's, say around seven o'clock?"

Ladesque crashed her fist against the counter. "Excuse me! Lawsuits and financial reports from 2010 and onward! I want them. NOW! Legally, they must remain public information."

"Try the legal department, then," the clerk huffed, pointing down the corridor.

~ * ~

"Pleased to meet you, Sally. I'm Angie," the woman behind the desk in the legal department said cheerfully. "Any public information on lawsuits would be in the annual reports. What year are we looking for?"

"From 2010 through 2013." Ladesque followed Angie to a massive filing cabinet. "Is there information that would *not* be public?"

"Lawsuits that were settled with a confidentiality agreement, such as, 'We'll pay you x number of dollars and you don't tell anyone and we don't go to court now or ever again.'" The clerk opened a drawer and rifled through the contents.

"What else would remain secret?"

"Lawsuits not yet settled." She pulled out three slick-covered reports. "Publishing information about cases still before the court would be seen as interfering with the legal process. Also, information about lawsuits that were dropped and lawsuits against individuals, such as directors or professors, wouldn't be published. It would violate their right to privacy. Here are the 2010 to 2013 annual reports. They should have the financial info about research grants and such that you're after, too."

Ladesque scoured the pages of the annual reports, which were obviously designed to impress supporters and potential investors. The *Financial Statements* made up a small part of the glossy production. Legal issues got even less coverage. A student had sued for falling on an icy sidewalk and some professor won his suit over loss of his prime parking spot, but there was no mention of Alice Jergens, nor of any lawsuit connected to the Human Sexuality Research Centre. There were six pages of tiny-typed donors and supporters of the university listed—several of them were pharmaceutical companies.

She recognized Phizenhessen out of Chicago—one of the major manufacturers of chemical birth control products before the crash of 2010 and before eunuchism took the glitter off their products. Since eunuchs proved to be disinclined to desire something they'd never have and parents felt obligated to love their daughters as they were rather than avenging what their daughters had lost, Phizenhessen had been slowly clawing its way back to prominence. She noted the phone number of the company. It might be worth a call. Perhaps Phizenhessen had intended to fund her mother's research—that could explain the *'rejected due to pending lawsuit'* comment on the proposal.

If she knew how to read the figures on the financial statements, perhaps she could uncover something more about this possibility. She approached the clerk. "Which numbers on here refer to privately-funded research projects?"

Angie flipped through the pages. "This page contains the financials specific to the university's research department. If you look under income…there. It's broken down into government grants, donations, funded research…There, that's the number."

"It doesn't say who funded the research?"

"That likely wouldn't show in the annual report. It would be in the audited financial statements, though."

"Where would I find them?"

"Try Administration."

Ladesque sighed in frustration. Going in circles was NOT her favourite pastime and the Admin receptionist was not her favourite lady. She had no choice, though. As she rushed back to Administration, the Phizenhessen name and logo kept reappearing in her mind. She searched her memory for the source of the familiarity. There'd been a news story about the pharmaceutical company's soaring stock values the night Paul had been in her kitchen watching eunuch, Tracy Spence wed football star, Avery Sell. Perhaps that's what she was recalling.

When Ladesque rushed back into the administration office, the secretary was turning off lights and struggling into her sweater. "Sorry, we're closed for the day," she snipped.

Suddenly Ladesque's mind translated Phizenhessen into the squiggles and lines of Pitman. She froze. That's why it was familiar. 'Phizenhessen', encrypted in shorthand, had appeared often on the pages of her mother's diary.

"No, please!" Ladesque begged. "I've come all the way from Colorado. And I have to catch my plane back tonight. I just need a bit of help. The audited financial statements, where would I find them?"

"In the safe, which is locked and can't be opened until tomorrow morning. Besides, you'd need expressed permission from the dean to look at that information."

"It's public information!"

"Not twenty-four seven, it isn't." The woman snapped off the last light and waved Ladesque out ahead of her. The click of the key in the lock behind Ladesque signalled an end to her search. Unless, the Harvard Alumni Association had something…

CHAPTER 19

Ladesque stood at the airport pay phone, tapping her fingers and counting her coins. If the Harvard Alumni receptionist didn't take her off hold soon, she was going to have to hang up or miss her plane. The annoying hold music stopped. "Have you been helped?" a soft voice asked.

"No, I've been holding—"

"Please deposit another dollar," a robotic voice interceded.

Ladesque continued talking as she fumbled with her change. "I'm looking for information on my mother, Alice Jergens. She graduated from Harvard in—"

"What kind of information?"

"I'm trying to track her employment history following—"

"There's a research fee that must be paid up front before we'll release any information we have on our alumni."

"You're kidding. A research fee?"

"Look, we lost all our records during the Crash and our archived copies turned out to be compromised as well. Along with most of the world, our budget was depleted trying to restore our lost data. We started charging for our information way back then and to this day it is one of our major fund raisers. Our scholarships—"

"I understand. How much is this research fee?"

"Commercial or governmental requests for information can range upward of a thousand dollars. Since you're family, it would cost a few hundred dollars, depending. If your mother were to request her file, it would cost nothing...if it turns out she is indeed, alumni."

"My mother can't request anything. She's dead."

"Oh. I'm sorry to hear that. We don't have any policy about special circumstances. I'm afraid I'd have to charge you the going rate. I'll need to receive a written request outlining the info you want and accompanied by a bank draft—"

Ladesque heard the general boarding call for her flight to Denver. "I'll get back to you," she said, slamming the receiver into the cradle.

She plugged a handful of quarters into the coin slot and dialled the number for Phizenhessen Pharmaceuticals. She was relieved when someone answered. "I'm looking for information on a research project

Phizenhessen was involved with around the time of the Great Crash. Who would I talk to?"

"What kind of research?"

"It was a project that was to have been subcontracted to McGill University Human Sexuality Research Centre."

"What is your interest in this project?"

"My mother, Alice Jergens, prepared the protocol and presentation to the University's Board of Governors. She died a while back and I was going through her things, trying to get to know her. I have a feeling this project was important to her."

"Most of our research is confidential," the secretary said. "However, because this dates back quite a while if you were to send a written request outlining your interest…"

A feeling of utter frustration seized Ladesque. It seemed the universe was conspiring to keep her mother's secrets from her. "I'll get my lawyer to do that," Ladesque shouted. "You can expect to hear from him via registered mail! Perhaps my interest has a whole bunch to do with the fact I'm a eunuch!"

She slammed the phone into the cradle. Two quarters tingled out the change chute.

Over the loudspeaker a feminine voice announced first in French and then in English, "Final boarding call for flight three eighty nine to Denver, Colorado…"

Ladesque cuddled up with her Pitman textbook during the flight home. She had it almost entirely memorized by the time the wheels of the plane hit the tarmac in Denver. Perhaps she wouldn't need the alumni information or lawsuit financials if she could decipher her mother's diary.

During the taxi ride home, she rehearsed in her mind unlocking her front door and running downstairs. She could see herself, feel herself, reaching into the second largest cardboard box and right on top, would be her mother's diary. She'd open it. The broken lock would dangle through her fingers of her right hand. She'd flip through the pages about her birth, her first tooth, graduating from kindergarten. Past her tenth birthday… to her teen years. To the cryptic writing. The squiggles and lines that had stymied her. She would read what happened after her thirteenth birthday. She'd find out her mother's thoughts about her sexless future. Perhaps she would learn how her dad felt. Perhaps…

Visualizing the future was an obsessive habit of hers, that got more detailed and repetitive the more emotional the circumstances. She'd pay the driver, rush up her front steps, unlock her front…

The taxi pulled to the curb. She passed the driver his fare and threw open the cab door. She would now dash up the walk, into her house, down the basement…open the diary. The driver coughed, his hand extended for the tip she'd forgotten. She shoved some more bills into his hand and bolted toward the house.

Once inside, the lights came on, a robot voice announced she had three telephone messages waiting, and then howled eerily.

Ladesque stopped. Her heart pounded. The howl meant her indoor security system had sensed an intruder while she'd been gone. She reached behind her for the doorknob, prepared to make a quick escape. Someone had broken in, bypassed the standard security alarms, but been caught by the customized motion sensors she'd programmed.

She'd always imagined phoning 911 if she ever heard that howl. But that had been when she had a job on the tenth floor. Emergency 911 would definitely not know how to deal with an intruder, a watched woman, and the FBI.

If she crept down the hall to her bedroom and then into her walk-in closet where the security system control panel was hidden, she could get more information, like the time of the intrusion. It was risky, though. For all she knew the intruder was still in her house. *What the hell do I do?*

Keeping her back to the wall, she cautiously inched to her bedroom and into her closet. She flicked on the light. Nothing looked out of place. She moved quickly now, shoving sweaters and skirts out of the way until she had her hands on the built-in metal cabinet that housed the brain of her security system. She entered the code and wrenched open the door. There was a small computer inside. She keyed in her password followed by the command to replay recently stored data. It was as unsettling as she'd feared.

The intruder had somehow bypassed her video surveillance but the high-tech motion-detectors she'd installed had captured movement and encoded it in a digital message. She flicked a few keys and the encrypted data dissolved into English. Someone had been in her house two hours ago and left shortly before her arrival. The intruder was likely a few inches under six feet tall and had visited every room in her house, including the basement.

She twirled around and nervously scanned her dresser, the night stand, her vanity. Her bed was made and un-mussed, just as she'd left it. The towels hung as they always did. The blinds were drawn, as she remembered leaving them. *What would an intruder be after?*

She had little of value in her house. As per policy, absolutely nothing from work ever made it into her home. She kept no cash, owned no jewellery and made do with cheap furnishings. The only place she stored passwords was in her memory.

She re-locked the control panel and slowly stepped out of the closet.

The street lights shining through her drapes gave the room an eerie, muted orange glow. She once more scanned her room, looking closely into the corners where shadows had seemed to move the first time her eyes had travelled by.

When Paul warned me I was a watched woman, is this what he meant? Perhaps he'd let her leave the country without hassle in order to have uninterrupted access to her house for the day. Maybe that's why he'd suggested she visit her home town. Had it been Paul or fellow FBI agents in her house? Were they looking for something to blackmail her? Something they could use to force her into biologically programming Skinner's Box?

Ladesque jumped when the phone in the kitchen jangled. Keeping her back to the wall she slithered back down the corridor. Everything looked right. Everything seemed the same as when she left. She would not have known from looking at her kitchen or her living room, her foyer or her bedroom that someone had been here.

Just as she reached it, the phone quit ringing. She stared at the receiver. Even though it would have been impossible for her to get the internet up and running securely, if she'd persisted on the tenth floor for a few more months, she'd have had telecommunications secure enough for companies to once again offer call display, cordless handsets, answering services, and basic cellular service.

Her tape-recording message machine was blinking. Before she could hit the play button, her phone began to ring again. Still not feeling safe from the intruder, and fearing the ringing phone was distracting her from due vigilance, she turned her back to it and walked to the basement stairs. It was dark and dreary down there. The furnace and plumbing and water tank made unpredictable noises, cast dark shadows and created great hiding spaces between them.

Although her sensors said the intruder was gone, like all others of her generation, she distrusted technology—even that of her own design. It seemed hackers were always a step ahead of the firewalls. Suppose the intruder had been aware of her secret security, over-ridden it and planted a false message that he was gone. Suppose he was actually still here. Suppose...?

She flicked on the stairwell light and slowly descended. Where the upstairs wall ended and the basement spindles began, she hunched down and peered through the rails. Her mother's boxes that she'd pulled from under the stairs still sat there.

She tried to remember how she'd left them. She recalled rushing downstairs to grab some books before catching the taxi to the airport. Had she left the boxes open, all of them, as they were now? Had she put the rejected research project proposal on the very top of the smallest box instead of back in the box from which it had come? Had she placed Rod McEwan's *Lonesome Cities* in the craft box upside down? No, definitely not.

She stumbled down the last three steps and frantically rushed toward the boxes. Her mother's personal diary with its broken lock and Pitman Shorthand entries simply had to still be there. It could not have been taken. She must get the chance to read it now that she knew how!

Upstairs, the message machine beeped, the telephone again jangled, the buzzer rang and the robot lady, once again, ever so patiently announced all these things to her.

CHAPTER 20

She found the diary at the very bottom of the box with her mother's craft supplies, confirming beyond a doubt an intruder had rummaged through the boxes. She clutched the diary to her heart and raced up the stairs.

Roach's voice blared through the intercom. "Ladesque! It's Roach." He was hammering on the door. "Come on. Open up. I know you're there! I have something for you. Something you'll like."

"Visitor is still at the door," the robot voice enunciated. "Last telephone ring before answering machine picks up."

She set the diary on the phone desk and let the echo of the phone's last jangle fade before she picked up the receiver and plugged in Paul's number. She had not consented to this kind of intrusion into her personal life, her home, her sacred belongings. No matter how important Paul and his project were, how could he justify this kind of—

"Paul!" she screamed as soon as he answered. "What gives you the right to do this to me? This is unforgivable! This is a total abuse of your powers! If you need to know something about me, all you have to do is ask! Have I ever given you any reason to doubt my credibility? Have I? I've had top security clearance since I left high school. My life's been an open book. This is unforgivable! How dare—"

"What are you talking about?" Paul finally broke in.

"I know you were in my house while I was gone. I know you were in my basement!"

"Hold it! Ladesque, hold it! What are you talking about? Someone was in your house?"

"Don't play lame with me. I have indisputable evidence—"

"It wasn't me, Ladesque. Listen! It wasn't me. It wasn't anyone from the FBI. This is serious. You might not be safe. Are you okay? The intruder's not still there? I'm coming over, Ladesque. I'm on my way."

"Are you sure it wasn't you?" Ladesque said. Her eyes once more roamed the corners and the shadows. "Who would it be if it wasn't you?" Had her questions in Montreal or her calls from the airport raised someone else's warning flags? *Are Phizenhessen or McGill or Harvard out to discover how much I know?*

"Perhaps this is…corporate espionage or some such. I'm coming over. We'll talk about it when I get there."

Ladesque hung up and hit the button to play back her three waiting telephone messages. Two of them were from Paul and one from Roach. All were asking where she was and begging her to call as soon as she got in.

"Ladesque?" Roach called through the speaker. "I'm not leaving until I talk to you. Please let me in."

She was more terrified than ever. What if Paul was telling the truth and had nothing to do with the break in? What if someone with much more sinister reasons had been in her home?

She commanded every light in the house to come on. Who had belonged to the feet that had walked her halls? Whose fingers had touched her things? Whose eyes had peered into her personal spaces? She shivered, picked up the diary and let Roach in. A huge, proud smile creased his face. "Gotcha something," he said. From behind his back he pulled a six pack of bottled beer.

Ladesque smiled lamely. "Black'ors beer," she said.

"No, Black Horse...oh, that's what you said?"

"Black'ors. It's brewed in Newfoundland and that's how they pronounce it."

"Newfoundland? Is that in Canada?"

"Yeah. Sort of. Don't worry. The beer qualifies as Canadian." Ladesque took the beer from Roach with her free hand and beckoned him in. Before closing the door, she scanned the street. It was empty of vehicles and people. Not even the grey sedan was in sight.

She watched bemused as Roach struggled to kick off his shoes. It took a minute or two of flailing before he got them free and then he had to bend and pull up his socks. He finally stood and turned his attention to her. He caught her eyes and smiled shyly. She grinned back.

Roach wiped his hair off his forehead and shifted awkwardly from foot to foot. "Here, let me," he finally said, reaching for the case of beer. "Where were you all day?

"I flew to Montreal."

"Montreal? How was your trip?"

"Unsuccessful." Ladesque carefully passed off the beer. "Frustrating." His shoulders relaxed, as if her voice was comforting. "Let's sit in the living room. Do you want a beer glass or shall we drink from the bottle?"

"Bottle's fine." He sauntered to the sofa ahead of her. It wasn't exactly a limp, just a little heavier thrust with his left leg, a little outturn of his left foot. With his thick waist and rounded hips and with the grey fleece of his jacket softly rolling with his gait, he reminded Ladesque of comforting cuddles in her mother's lap, years ago—in the rocking chair.

She wished that comfort could again be hers. Strong, soft, warm arms around her, erasing all things bad about herself and her world.

He'd sunk into the sofa and snapped open two beer before she realized she was staring at him, still clutching her mother's diary to her heart. Roach coughed nervously and held out a Black'ors.

"Please believe me, I wasn't really staring at you. I was just deep in thought." She accepted the brew and plopped in the upholstered side chair. "I'm exhausted. It's been a long and stressful few days." She laid the diary on her lap and sucked back a stream of the distinctively musky beer. It wasn't her favourite but it was cold and wet.

"What happened?"

Her life was not at all the life she'd imagined as a young girl. None of it. Despite her planning, her education, her goals. Despite her best intentions. Fate, visitors, intruders were always disrupting things. Like the cancer that took her mom, the accident that claimed her dad. Just like Paul taking her hand as she stepped out of the tenth floor elevator. Just like tonight—

She set the diary on her lap and took another swig. When she leaned forward to put bottle on the coffee table, the diary fell open in her lap. She glanced down. It was the page where her mother announced her birth in clear plain English.

"What happened to stress you out?" Roach repeated.

"Did you know my mother was a researcher at McGill University's Human Sexuality Centre in Montreal?"

"Did you just find that out? Does that bother you?"

"I was going through some of her papers the other day. No, it doesn't bother me. What bothers me is that I couldn't find any information on—"

"Visitor at the front door," Robot Lady said.

"Ladesque!" Paul hammered frantically. "It's me, Paul. Let me in. Ladesque!"

Ladesque set the diary on the coffee table and commanded the door to open. Paul barged in. "Are you all right?" he asked breathlessly. "I heard a man's voice..."

"It's just Roach," Ladesque said.

"He's the intruder?" Paul stepped toward Roach, anger flashing in his eyes.

"No!" Ladesque quickly stood and rushed between the men. "Roach isn't the intruder. He's just visiting. Brought me some Black'ors."

"I can leave," Roach offered.

"You can and you will," Paul growled. Roach squirmed off the sofa and ducked past Paul.

Ladesque chased after him. "Don't leave, please. At least finish your beer."

Roach glanced quickly at Paul and then slunk toward the door. "I might not be an intruder," he said, struggling into his shoes, "but someone can sure make me feel like one."

Ladesque looked to one man and then the other. "Paul, why are you being such an ass? Roach, stay."

"It's best he leaves," Paul said. "You and I have much to talk about."

"It's okay, Ladesque." Roach waved Ladesque back to the living room. "I'll let myself out."

She flopped onto the sofa and the front door slammed. "I can't believe you did that, Paul. I've never been so humiliated! How dare you treat *my* guests in *my* house that way!"

Paul chuckled. "It's either him or me and I'll tell you now, if it were *my* life in danger, it wouldn't be Roach I'd want around to protect me."

"Why not?"

"He hardly has the ability to put on his shoes, let alone defend someone."

"Don't insult my friends! I'm not going to put up with it. You're so uncouth!" Her words were tumbling out faster than her thoughts formed. "At least Roach loves me!"

Her face burned with embarrassment. "Maybe not love," she hastily corrected. "But he cares about me."

"I care about you," Paul said softly.

He was staring down at her as if he did care. As if…His mesmerizing, magnetic eyes searched her face. Magnetic. His entire body was magnetic. She felt compelled to stand. As if reading her mind, he reached for her hands and pulled her to him.

Smoothly and without effort he placed her hands on his hips and wrapped his arms about her shoulders. He was so close. He was so warm. His eyes were still on her, his breath was sweet. His lips lush and approaching as if he desired her. As if….he loved her.

"I'm sorry." He abruptly pushed her away. "That was totally inappropriate." He strolled to the window, leaving her in a wash of cold air.

"How much do you care about me?" Ladesque asked. His back was to her, his head bowed, his hands jammed in his pockets. The hot feelings that had once engorged her crotch were now diluted and warm, spreading effusively throughout her body. A peaceful, beautiful feeling filled her heart and her breasts and her brain. Perhaps this was the difference between lust and love.

"Not at all that way," he said firmly. "It was just rogue male instincts."

"Not at all an invitation to mutually share the pleasures of body parts?" she asked. *Am I falling in love?*

"Not at all."

He was likely telling the truth; it was lust not love on both their parts. If he loved her he would not have considered her disposable, unattached to this world and its people—a prime candidate to crawl into his computer and disappear—unnoticed.

He finally turned to her and pointed to the side chair. "May I sit? We need to talk."

"Sure," she said, curling up on the sofa.

"Tell me about the intruder." He put his feet up on the coffee table, comfortable. Like he was at home. Like he belonged to her.

"My security system didn't catch anything on video but recorded motion starting two hours before I arrived home and quitting an hour and a half later."

"Why no video?"

Ladesque shrugged. "I imagine whoever it was, knew how to bypass the cameras."

"Perhaps it was just a glitch in your system? A dead battery in the camera? A dusty lens?"

"No, the cameras are working fine. I can show you video of you arriving if you wish."

"A glitch in the motion sensors? They were simply detecting shadows from the clouds moving across the sun? A flock of birds flying past your window? The wind—"

"No. Someone was definitely here. They rifled through the boxes of my mother's papers and books that are stored in the basement. I haven't noticed anything missing, though."

"This worries me. I've ordered additional surveillance of your home."

"Who do you think it might be?"

"At first I was afraid someone who knew about your involvement in our quantum computer project was out to stop you, abduct you, bribe you, intimidate you. However, the evidence suggests the intruder knew you weren't home. I suppose they could have been looking for something with which to blackmail you, but if they were rifling through your mother's papers, it suggests another motive."

"Like what?"

"I'll make you a deal, Ladesque." Paul set his feet on the floor and leaned toward her. "I've been researching your mother, too. You tell me what you know and I'll tell you what I know. Deal?"

"What do you know about her?"

"You go first," Paul said.

"I can't go first. I didn't find out anything. It's as if she disappeared from the world along with the internet in the aftermath of the Great Crash." Ladesque's eyes darted to the diary on the coffee table between them. When she realized Paul noticed, she instinctively grabbed the diary and hugged it to her chest. Too late, she realized her mistake.

"What's that?" Paul asked.

"Nothing…my mother's diary. It's written in code. I haven't yet deciphered it."

"How long do you need to decipher it?"

"Not long. I've been wanted to do it since I got home, but life keeps interrupting."

"I'll let you read it." Paul lounged back in his chair. "Ladesque, I'm not being cagey or secretive. I could likely tell you most of what's in there, but there's a lot of stuff it's best you learn straight from your mother's own words. Personal stuff. Things you might find upsetting."

"Upsetting?"

"I'll go into the kitchen and watch some TV while you read. Call me when you're done."

CHAPTER 21

Ladesque was wiping tears from her eyes when Paul returned to the room. "My mother sacrificed her life for me." She softly closed the diary and pressed it to her lips.

"That she did," Paul agreed. He sat down opposite her and folded his hands in his lap. "In more ways than one."

"She loved me the way I was but felt I'd been cheated."

"I'm not privy to her personal feelings about the situation, but I did uncover the legal papers—her lawsuit against Phizenhessen."

"Her passionate pursuit of justice was not so much because I was rendered a eunuch by their birth control pharmaceuticals, but more because the company ignored research predicting this would happen and then covered up their culpability."

"Yes, that was the gist of the lawsuit."

"Which she dropped."

"I understand there was an out-of-court settlement."

"Mom offered to drop the lawsuit in exchange for being allowed to participate in a study of a pill developed to reverse the damage. She not only wrote the protocol for the study, but participated in it. It may have been the test drugs that caused her cancer."

"I didn't know that part. The settlement was secret."

"There's other stuff," Ladesque said quietly. She fanned the pages of the diary with her thumb.

"Personal stuff? We can talk about it or not. It's up to you."

"A year or two after I failed my pheromone test, Mom injected me with an experimental serum. The injection was slow acting, akin to genetic engineering. The expected return of libido didn't happen and the trials were stopped."

She didn't tell him that after those trials her mother had frantically pursued a half-dozen additional studies, none successful. Nor did she tell him that data trickling in from the initial drug trial, indicated that following a delay of up to twenty years, the desired effects might appear.

"I know."

"What do you know?" The most devastating news, she also chose not share—her libido was temporary; it would last only a few weeks.

"Commit to the project and I'll tell you."

Ladesque thumbed through the diary. Her mother had mentioned lobbying on social network sites for answers and a solution and money. For justice. For more trials. "I'm not ready yet to commit," Ladesque said. "I'm still trying to understand all this. I need more information. As the diary progressed and mom got sicker, she made fewer and fewer entries."

"Do you want to go through more of her papers? I can turn over the legal stuff I found."

"I'd like that. I'd also like to try again to find her on the archived internet pages."

Paul sighed. "I was afraid you'd say that."

"Why does that make you afraid?"

"I uncovered a second legal trail. Your dad's accident may not have been so accidental—"

"What? Are you saying Dad's death was a murder?"

"After your mother's death, he decided since he wasn't a party to the out-of-court settlement, he could pursue a lawsuit against Phizenhessen on your behalf. He also managed to get a criminal inquiry launched. Your father died before the lawsuit reached the courts. His death was investigated as suspicious but the whole thing fell apart with the internet crash. As with so many legal cases back then, the prosecutors believed it would be difficult to convince a jury evidence hadn't been altered or affected by hackers. The investigations of both Phizenhessen and your father's death were dropped."

"Both my parents gave their life for me?" Ladesque wailed.

Paul stood and walked toward the door. "Some say there's no stronger relationship than that of a father and daughter." He slipped on his shoes and opened the door. "I'll send someone for you tomorrow to take you to the tenth floor internet archives."

CHAPTER 22

Ladesque gave up searching for her mother on the social networks. Her diary had said she was an avid participant, an online activist lobbying for justice. However, Ladesque couldn't find her name. Likely because, if her mother had signed a confidentiality agreement, she would've had to disguise her identity if she was taking Phizenhessen to task on the internet.

Ladesque reluctantly admitted she was not clever enough to unmask that identity. Google searches for asexuality in the medical or scientific context netted very little—apparently not a lot was known about the condition in the early part of the third millennium. A search for Phizenhessen resulted in a standard corporate website, full of the usual promotional materials and pictures of people radiating health and well being. Not surprisingly, given her father's aversion to high-tech, search results for him were limited to sites that listed his name but wanted payment for more info—ancestry.com, LinkedIn—archived sites that were no longer live, their information frozen.

Ladesque sighed and peered out the side of her eye at the escort Paul had provided her. She was surprised to see him still alert, his eyes watching her fingers flash about the keyboard. It must be dull to watch someone for hours when you couldn't see the monitor.

She plugged *Pitman Shorthand* into the Google search engine just for the hell of it, and was surprised to discover both the text books and online courses were still available in 2010 from Amazon. She wondered who'd used shorthand when it seemed technology must surely have made it obsolete by then. Discouraged at her lack of success but not wanting to abandon what might be her only chance to find her mother online, she scrolled listlessly through the Pitman results.

Bingo! On the eighth page of results, links to Alice Pitman on Twitter and Facebook appeared. The truncated entries both also contained the word Phizenhessen.

Ladesque straightened and her fingers flew across the keyboard. She dug deep behind the chatter, following link after link. Reading bio after bio. Searching both supporters and detractors. She felt a hand on her shoulder, and jumped. Roach was staring down at her with his crooked little grin.

"Still here?" he asked.

"Hands off her!" her guard warned, quickly rising.

"It's okay—" Ladesque started. The man was instantly on Roach, swatting his hand from her shoulder and shoving him toward the exit. Startled, Ladesque rose and rushed toward the men. "We're friends. It's okay. I used to work here—"

"I have my orders," the guard growled. He had Roach by the collar. "Whoever the hell you are, I suggest you leave."

"Sure." Roach took several quick steps backward toward the door. "No problem. Just was…going…asking if she wanted a coffee. Fine." He turned on his heel. "I'm outta here," he muttered.

Ladesque turned to the guard. "What are your orders?" she demanded.

"Sit!" The guy waved her toward the computer. "Or, are you finished?"

"No, I'm not finished. What are your orders?"

"To keep you safe."

"Oh." Ladesque slowly walked back to the computer. "I thought you were here to spy on me or something. Keep me from running off, perhaps. I thought I was…like a watched woman."

"That you are." The guy once more settled his bulk into the chair in the corner.

Ladesque resumed her search. She discovered all was not as her mother had said. Diminished libido was a common side effect of all hormonal contraceptives and therefore, it hadn't been blatant disregard for facts that had led researchers to dismiss the results of the testing of their new drug. In fact, reduced sex drive was a common side effect of many medications, notably the popular antidepressants of the day.

Additionally, scientific articles suggested it had not simply been unfettered greed that had driven Phizenhessen to develop the new contraceptive, but rather its desperate search for a contraceptive that carried less risk of causing cancer and heart attacks than the estrogen and progesterone contraceptives that had made history in the last half of the 1900's.

Such evidence had not swayed her mother. From the time Ladesque was conceived, her mother seemed terrified a generation of asexual women was about to bless the world—and her child was going to be among them. She had demanded access to the raw data behind Phizenhessen required trials for FDA approval and was hounding the experts to recognize what was happening, and the media to report on it.

It must have been just before Ladesque hit her teens, after the fallout from the Great Crash had killed the internet that people began to realize asexuality was a permanent and genetically transferable side effect from the popular Phizenhessen drug.

Even though her mother's worst fears were realized with Ladesque's pubescent pheromone test, if Phizenhessen's motives were as magnanimous and benign as it appeared, it was obvious to Ladesque why her mother would have opted to drop her lawsuit. What wasn't so obvious was why her father later became involved. Did he have information to refute the arguments by Phizenhessen?

She made notes of websites visited, printed off some of the data she'd uncovered and then hit the off button. The computer stuttered for a moment and then all was quiet. "I'm finished," she said, gathering her belongings.

~ * ~

"What do you know about my father and where did you find the information?" Ladesque asked Paul.

He was lounging in his cushy office chair, appearing as if at any moment he'd put his feet on his desk. He was so good looking.

"As an FBI agent, I have access to police reports and legal documentation." He motioned her to sit.

"How close did the investigators come to confirming his accident was not accidental?" The chairs in his office were incredibly comfortable. She wondered if there was something about the fabric that drew out all the tension in her muscles.

"They were close, just shy of proving a motive."

"What was the suspected motive?"

"Prosecutors wanted to link his death to the lawsuit he'd launched against Phizenhessen. Phizenhessen insisted all research records were lost or tainted in the Great Crash. Without evidence your father had independent incriminating information, it would be hard to prove Phizenhessen had any reason to want him dead."

"But I found an archived copy of the original raw data from the research trials!"

"It would be difficult to prove it had not been compromised by the Crash."

"But McGill says all their research records were meticulously stored as hard copy. Wouldn't that have been a standard procedure for all research labs?"

Paul shrugged. He straightened and leaned across his desk. His eyes were on her. Warm. Sympathetic. Mesmerizing. "At one point, a request for a search warrant on the Phizenhessen lab was filled out, but it was never submitted. Likely because a judge gave a verbal denial. Phizenhessen insisted all their research records were destroyed."

His eyes were so intense. She almost fell into them, but she didn't.

Something…something warned her he was using his seductive stare to conceal a secret.

She closed her eyes to hide her suspicions, hoping he'd believe she was merely swooning under his attentive, liquid gaze.

"What are you thinking?" he asked.

"Why do you look at me like that?" she asked.

"What do you mean?"

"You look like you want to swallow me whole. That you'd love to wrap me in your arms. That you want to protect me, love me, mate with me." She opened her eyes.

"I do?" He chuckled. His chair creaked as he rocked back in it. He stuck his pen in his mouth and smiled at her, amused. "I've told you before, I look into your eyes to see if you're telling the truth."

He was backlit from the low winter sun in the window behind him. Nothing accentuated symmetry more than a silhouette. He was so perfect. She ought to just forget her suspicions. If he was hiding something from her, it was likely for her own good. He was in the intelligence industry, her boss—of course he had secrets. It didn't mean they were ominous ones.

Still—

"I'm not at all satisfied with the results of my research," Ladesque said. "Having said that, I'm pretty sure I'm going to refuse to participate in the quantum computer project. I've come to feel a deep connection to my world and an all-consuming need to discover the truth about my parents. I'm convinced that once I discover that truth, there will be things I need to do to get them justice."

"You will not be allowed to do that, Ladesque." His voice was so low and powerful it vibrated her ribs.

"I won't be allowed to?"

He neither leaned forward nor drew back. He sat still and impassive. "You have totally overestimated your autonomy." He spoke so quietly, she felt compelled to lean toward him. "Listen to me—I repeat, you will not be allowed to do that. Do you understand?"

"What *will* I be allowed to do?"

"You will be allowed to participate in the project."

"And, should I refuse?"

"You will not refuse." He rose and strode around his desk. He pulled her from her chair and drew her to him. He smelled wonderful. Rustic. She caught a whiff of sweet breath as he bent to kiss her. His lips were hot—swollen. His tongue searched. *What is he doing?*

His hands slid down her shoulders—to her waist, her butt. He ground her to him, his hardness pushing, throbbing, against her tummy, his knee pressing her crotch. He truly was going to swallow her whole—merge with her. He laid his lips on hers and for a long time they swayed together.

"That's just a trial run," he said when he finally pulled back, "of what you will find in Skinner's Box." He didn't apologize for his kiss this time. *It's as if he knows I'm not a eunuch.*

"Skinner's Box?" She licked her lips, his sweetness still clung there. She might as well enjoy it because according to her mom's diary, these feelings would not last.

"Do you know why we chose that code name?" Paul asked, as if they'd been talking academia all along " *Maybe he doesn't know.*

"Skinner?" *How could he not know?*

"B.F. Skinner, Paul continued, "was an American behaviourist who designed a box with a lever that when pressed would release treats to lab rats. He used rewards and punishment to analyze their behaviour. He was one of the first scientists to quantify, measure, alter, and predict behaviour—"

If he doesn't know how I'm feeling, what happened to his demand for mutual desire and consent?

"I can recite Skinner's life by rote," Ladesque interrupted. "He was seen by many as the father of behavioural science. Prior to Skinner, knowledge about behaviour was restricted to philosophy. He placed the very essence of humanity into the laboratory—bringing it under the scrutiny of science."

"You're right, Ladesque. His behavioural theories reduced human nature to the level of rats." *What are you reducing me to?* "Although it was not popular science to some, curiosity about ourselves overcame objections. Since then, scientists have used all tools available to analyze brain chemistry, construction, and processes in their attempts to decipher human intelligence and behaviour. Until now, however, we didn't have the mathematically definition of that humanness that we needed in order to digitize it. Our efforts at creating artificial intelligence, while amazing, always fell flat in the flexibility and creativity departments."

"But now?"

"The next great breakthrough is about to happen. We now have the necessary mathematical equations to digitize the chemistry that underlies both our intelligence and our behaviour, although they have yet to be proven and yet to be computerized."

"You're telling me too much. You're assuming I've agreed—"

"Oh, you've agreed, Ladesque. You've agreed." He grabbed her once more for a kiss. With his lips glued to hers, he walked her out of his office and into the hallway, his knee playing touch and go with the swelling between her legs and his hands tracing circles on her lower back.

When Paul finally pulled away, she gulped for air. She now understood. It was crystal clear how sexuality created, deepened and destroyed relations. Ended careers, toppled nations. Launched a thousand ships. Preserved the species. *What am I willing to do, to sacrifice in order to keep my sexual feelings alive?*

"It appears you are still quite curious about sex," Paul said.

"I can't imagine," she panted, "how merging with a computer can compare—"

"Oh, it's not a comparison you'll find in Skinner's Box." Paul clasped her hands in his. "It's much better than that. You'll find the tools to genetically modify your femininity—preserve it. Enhance it. Repair the damage done to you by the drugs. When you come back to me, Ladesque, you will be designed as you ought to have been from the start. Hot blooded, eager, able." She stood on her tiptoes, reaching for another kiss, but he dropped her hands and turned away. "Don't ever try to tell me again," he said as he headed for the catwalk, "that you will not do this project."

He's an arrogant ass.

CHAPTER 23

December 10, 2035

Today her two week reprieve was up, but Ladesque had no intention of wandering back to work. She would not give in to the burning between her legs and Paul's asinine prediction she wouldn't dare decline the project.

She stared sullenly out her kitchen window. Somewhere beyond the city lights were the Rockies, with all their power and secrets. Somewhere, way up high were the stars, with all their secrets. They knew from whence they were born and when and why. Soon, very soon, according to Paul, those secrets would be unveiled—when Ladesque laid herself down to sacrifice her chemistry to Skinner's Box.

She had an inkling about those secrets. Traditional science had been slowly unearthing the relationships between time and space, the past and present, and energy and matter. Man was close to comprehending that ultimate link—between quanta and the big bang, between everything that is and that ever was. The singular identity that is matter, antimatter and dark matter.

She wondered if the ancients had known those secrets. What had sparked the biblical writers to declare God was the Alpha and the Omega, the beginning and the end, the everything and the nothing? Had the philosophers known all along that time bites its own tail and becomes infinity?

She wondered if the new science she created in Skinner's Box would also become a new religion, a source of comfort and inspiration. Or, would it steal hope from humanity when the knowledge it created dashed man's belief in an external and very finite God who had eyes to watch and a heart to care.

By merging with the computer, Ladesque would be merging man and machine, energy and matter, science and religion, the cosmos and the quanta, forever and never, the beginning and the end.

She sighed. A different kind of merging was filling her thoughts, an all-consuming physical kind. The merging holding her prisoner to this project was Paul's promise of what was to come. She was willing to risk her life, her mind, her god-knows-what for sex. A tumble in the hay. Paul's hot lips against hers—his penis where it ought to be, huge and hard and thrusting, to ease the desire that was driving her crazy.

It was no longer sating to rub herself to climax. It simply left her feeling empty, desiring more, seeking to fill the empty space that sucked on nothing. She was consumed with physical desires, so much so she'd been totally distracted from her search for answers about her mother and father.

She shook her head and rose. Sometimes if she paced, she forgot about Paul and his promises. Sometimes if she read—she picked up her mother's diary and flipped the pages. She'd been through it a dozen times. Had it memorized.

Something out her front window caught her eye and she remembered she was being watched and someone had broken into her house and rifled through her possession. She never had discovered anything missing. Who had set foot in her house while she was gone and what had he or she been looking for?

Had it been someone from Phizenhessen looking for her mother's notes about the drug that went wrong? That didn't seem likely, since the diary had been tossed aside. Although it could have been photographed before being left for her. *The intruder would've had to know Pitman, though, to know if the diary was safe to leave with me.* It wasn't likely a person could have broken the Pitman code during the short time in her basement, especially when the textbook was with her in Montreal.

Had someone been seeking information on the Skinner's Box Project? Had someone from her eunuch sisterhood broken in, convinced she was a traitor, a danger to the society? And then she remembered her father and his 'accident'. Perhaps the important clues to her entire mystery rested in *his* papers, not her mother's.

When her father died, she'd been the executor of his will and sole heir. She'd examined his papers again and again as she'd worked through his investments and the remnants of her mother's affairs, which hadn't yet been settled at the time of his death. She'd scrutinized his legal papers, his life insurance policy, his income tax returns. Nothing had seemed suspicious.

She doubted he kept a diary—men didn't. But perhaps he had a day-timer, a to-do list—something wherein he'd scribbled personal notes. All his papers were in her safe, a low-tech key-locked fire-proof chamber concealed behind a stone on her imitation fireplace chimney.

She'd been in there just weeks ago to get her passport, but it was never easy remembering exactly which cultured rock it was hidden behind. She dug the key out of her purse and ran her finger along the grout lines until her nail slipped into a crack between the stones. In moments, she had the safe open and was rummaging through the familiar contents.

There was a stack of Canadian hundred dollar bills wrapped with an elastic—the same way she'd found them in her father's safe. If it had been American bills, she'd have assumed her father had kept them for his international travels—it was much easier to convert American money abroad than Canadian.

However, she couldn't think of a reason why he'd have several thousand dollars in Canadian cash. Perhaps it was a payment received for a cash deal of some sort he'd not had time to deposit before his untimely death. Or perhaps, he hadn't deposited it in order to avoid having to pay taxes on it, although that seemed unlikely. A few thousand dollars would not have put her father in a significantly higher tax bracket.

She shoved the money aside and thumbed through the papers. She remembered most of them. A small black-covered coil notebook caught her eye. She drew it to her, flipped it open and fanned the pages. Most had doodles on them.

She paused on one. It was a design of straight lines forming triangles and squares, very similar to the Phizenhessen logo. She looked at the writing beneath it, tiny and nearly illegible. "Renew passport' it said. She pulled out her father's passport. It had been renewed a month before he'd died. The only travel-stamp in it was one to the U.S. and back.

Her father travelled all over the world with his business—there was nothing unusual about his passport or the travel stamp. She flipped through the notebook. There were phone numbers jotted down, grocery lists, dates and times. It was like he kept this book by his phone and jotted things down as people called or as they came to him.

She looked at the last page. It had the address and phone number for the Canadian Embassy in Washington D.C.–perhaps that, too, was work-related. International trade and travel was always made easier if one had strong diplomatic relationships. Beneath that he'd written 'C.H.' and drawn an arrow to the name Charlie which was heavily underlined and circled.

She pulled out a small accordion folder in which he'd kept his will and other important papers. She thumbed through the pockets. It was all as she remembered. She shoved it all back in the safe. What now?

Then she remembered his rickety turn-of-the-millennium personal laptop. Perhaps it contained something. She recalled seeing it on the floor of her closet beneath several pairs of shoes. She believed she'd set it there the day of the funeral after trying unsuccessfully to turn it on. The battery had been dead and the cord connection kept failing.

She rushed to her closet and pulled out the old Dell *Lenovo*. Its model year likely dated back a half-dozen years or so before the Crash. Her father had never been one to keep up with change and after the Great Crash, none of that mattered anymore anyway. She plugged it in and waited, not overly optimistic it would awake. Surprisingly, this time the old computer came to life and stayed on.

It was going to be a long night and not just because of the ancient technology; she'd have a lot of data to go through. Computers around the time of the crash held astounding memory capacity. Her task would be worse than looking for a needle in a haystack—at least when one was looking for a needle in a haystack, one knew it was a needle one was looking for.

Since there'd been no external disks, thumb drives, or other such data storage devices amongst her father's possessions, she had to assume any digitally recorded information about his search for the truth about her asexuality would be on the Lenovo hard drive.

It took her a while to get used to the quaint keyboard and mouse and the ancient Windows operating system, but she soon found the search feature and plugged in the word 'asexuality'. She asked for a search of the entire computer—all drives and folders. The dog-seeker wagged his tail and set to work.

Ladesque got up and made herself a strong cup of coffee.

It was a while before the search was complete. She opened the first document. "Since I wasn't a party to Alice's lawsuit…" she read and her heart leapt. *Does the fact Dad wasn't a party to that initial lawsuit mean he accepted me as I was?* That pleasant thought was fleeting, lasting only until she finished the sentence. There were only legal reasons he hadn't joined her mother's suit, not emotional ones.

Day was lightening the horizon when she wiped her eyes and finally shut off the computer. She could not believe she'd been at the centre of the far-reaching conspiracy her father had chronicled. A conspiracy that went beyond the economics of the pharmaceutical industry, beyond birth control gone wrong. Super secret medical experiments, funded by government itself, her government—the Canadian government. She was pretty sure she now knew whose agent had been snooping through her things.

She slapped the laptop closed and shivered from fatigue, cold and fear. No wonder the best of her security had not been able to stop the intruder—it was hard to out-manoeuvre the unlimited resources of a government. However, as was so often the case, it was the obvious and the low-tech that had stymied the intruder in his search—a stack of shoes atop an ancient laptop on the floor of a closet.

She did not know what to do with the information she now possessed, other than protect it at all costs.

The fact her dad's computer had been low-tech even for its model year added value and credence to its contents. The old Lenovo did not contain a card to enable internet connection so nobody could complain the data stored on it had been corrupted by the hackers behind the Great Crash. Everything it contained was uncontaminated truth. Her father made note of that fact, several times in his correspondence as he strived to get people to listen to his story.

Contrary to her initial hope her father had not minded her asexuality, she discovered he'd been searching for the truth about her 'affliction' (as he called it) before most even knew there was a truth to be searched for. Before she'd hit ten, before the Great Crash, when a generation of asexual women was just a whispered possibility, her dad had been hunting down those to blame. His reasons for not joining her mother's lawsuit were wrapped up in the legalities of him being out of country at the time and had nothing to do with his acceptance of her asexuality.

The government, he maintained, had collaborated with Phizenhessen to design a drug to inhibit female sexual feelings. According to her father's research, some scientists suggested this would lower the crime rate by reducing pheromone-induced testosterone-driven competitive aggression by males. He didn't note his feelings about that research, only that the report had gone before government officials. Ladesque assumed the authors of that report were males; it wasn't likely female researches would have blamed the female anatomy for the bad behaviour of men. However, most government officials at that time had been male as well. Perhaps it had made sense to them.

Reports from economists had predicted a positive effect on Canada's work force and pointed to a lucrative market for such a drug in emerging nations. Through reports and emails her father had scanned into his laptop, it appeared social scientists of the day had convinced governmental officials nations with an asexual female population would be more vulnerable to manipulation by both their leaders and wealthier nations—such as Canada. They predicted such countries would jump at the chance to buy a product that would presumably lower their birthrates as well as stabilize their labour forces.

She learned from her father's extensive personal missives that even though her mother had never suspected political involvement, he'd come to believe the government had felt threatened when she began to chat on the social networks. Her death had been ruled natural causes but her father suspected otherwise. He believed the experimental drugs she'd agreed to test had been purposely tampered with—laden with carcinogens. She found little hard evidence in his computer to back his suppositions, but he ardently believed he was right. Given his inability to get either government or industry to hand over information to disprove his theories, Ladesque became convinced, along with him, that he'd been right.

He'd sniffed out the trail that led from the laboratory into the political arena. To get the secret government reports that he needed, his records suggested he stopped at nothing—including threats and bribes. He wanted to uncover who the scientist was that ran the trials that killed his wife. He'd uncovered the initials C.H. and the name Charlie. He'd been so very close to proving they were one and the same and very sure he was going to sue the hell out of the man.

He'd carefully outlined everything—meetings, names, dates, notes. He'd scanned in pages and pages of hard copy research and correspondence. His chronicle contained digital photos, graphs, spreadsheets.

Initially, he'd tried legitimate means, such as requesting information through Canada's FOIP—Freedom of Information and Privacy legislation. His requests sat unfilled, the government claiming the Great Crash had wiped out all such records. When he'd taken his suspicions to the media, the story interested them but they believed the government's assertion that all records were lost. To strengthen his credibility he hauled out what was then recently-released top secret documents outlining experiments with mind altering drugs such as LSD that government scientists had secretly performed on unwitting citizens in the mid-1900's.

"Although we find your story interesting and well-researched," read one letter from a journalist, *"without proof of Government involvement, the risk of a lawsuit is too high. As our resources are severely limited, we're not able to pursue that proof."* Others said much the same, in less straight forward ways. Nobody believed the proof existed.

That's when her dad started going covert—hiring private investigators to gather unsavory personal information on bureaucrats. He used everything from affairs, to illicit drug use, even a daughter's juvenile criminal record to blackmail people into helping him in his search. He went after more than a dozen bureaucrats and their underlings and had some success in forcing them to cough up records, or point him to those who had could, or reveal weaknesses in the system he could exploit.

In the months before his death, he'd used her mother's entire $1 million life-insurance payout chasing down the truth. However, just hours after he'd typed in the most telling details of the illicit government experiments, he'd died.

Ladesque stumbled to the bathroom. Just inside the door, she caught sight of her reflection in the vanity mirror. Her red eyes with rimmed with dark circles, her face, grey. She looked terrified. Appalled. Betrayed by her government. By science. By corporate profits.

On the other hand…

Thoughts laden with emotion buzzed in her mind, circled back through her past, shot into the future and returned. If she'd found all this out before the first time she'd felt that warm rush in her crotch on the catwalk over the textile plant, would she have understood the reasons behind her father's corrupt activities? Behind her mother's pursuit of justice? Behind her father risking his career, reputation—his life all to bring to light the truth?

Would she even have cared?

She tumbled into bed and pulled the duvet over her head. Her parents should not have risked anything for her. She'd been fine. Her life had been unravelling as it should. She'd been okay. She had not needed sex. Instantly, she slept.

CHAPTER 24

Ladesque's head was pounding and the sun was streaming in her window when she awoke to the ringing phone. She squeezed her eyes shut, licked her lips, and swallowed. The ringing continued—a nerve-wracking, incessant jangling she somehow knew had been going on long before she'd wakened. The robot lady's voice came and went as a jumble of dream images circled in her mind. Visions of sinister invaders with maple leafs, faulty brakes, twisted metal. Coffins cradling her terrified parents.

"One more ring before the answering machine picks up," the robot lady said. Ladesque twisted in bed and reached for the receiver on her nightstand.

"Ladesque?" Paul asked before she'd said a word. "What the hell's going on? Why aren't you answering the phone? Are you okay? I was about to send in the SWAT team."

"I'm not okay," she mumbled. "Definitely not okay." She was dozing again as she talked; her parents' ghostly whispers were demanding she avenge their deaths and bring them justice.

"What's the matter? Are you sick?"

"I'll call you back."

"Don't you dare hang up!"

"I'm not okay, Paul. I was up all night. I'm ill. I have a migraine. I need to sleep. What time is it?"

"It's after noon. You're dehydrated—I can tell by your thick voice. You need to get up and get a drink and something to eat."

"Don't tell me what I need—"

"I'm coming over." The phone went dead. Ladesque replaced it on the cradle and slowly swung her feet to the floor. She'd never felt so alone in life. She had all this information, these terrible, dark secrets and didn't know what to do with them.

She traipsed to the bathroom, splashed water on her face, scrubbed her eyes, and ran a comb through her tangled curls. She looked as ill as she felt. Her eyes were dark holes in a pale, pale face. Fever spots reddened her cheekbones. Her lips were dry and cracked. Her tongue, thick and grey.

She plucked her toothbrush from the charger and iced it with Crest Supreme. It hummed and droned as she scrubbed at her teeth and her tongue. Her head pulsed in reaction and her stomach groaned. She retched into the sink—first only toothpaste but quickly followed by bile.

Each heave made her head pound louder, harder and more painfully. It took several minutes before her stomach settled enough for her to wash out the sink. She rinsed her mouth and again turned on her toothbrush. Hoping to curb her gag reflex, this time she was much less generous with the toothpaste.

She rinsed the peppermint taste from her mouth and took a small sip of water. It felt good on her lips and tongue, but travelled hard and cold down her oesophagus and settled like a river rock in her gut. The door bell rang.

"What's the matter? You look like hell warmed over," Paul said.

"I'm nauseated, have a splitting headache, was rudely awaken from a sound sleep, and I haven't yet had a coffee. Many more things are the matter. Do you want to hear them all?" She motioned him in.

"Take two Advil gels. I'll make us some brew." He headed to the kitchen.

She padded back down the hall to her room and rousted out the headache medication. She wondered if the capsules would make it past her swollen and dry tongue. And, if they did, would they stay in her belly or crawl back out? She clasped them in her hand and returned to the kitchen. She'd swallow them with her coffee—caffeine had a therapeutic effect on her migraines.

When she spotted Paul in the dinette with her dad's computer open in front of him, she cursed herself for her carelessness. "What are you doing?" She rushed forward. It wasn't too late—the computer was still struggling to come to life, its monitor yet blank. She slammed the laptop closed.

"This laptop is an antique. It interests me," Paul said.

"It's MY antique. Hands off."

"Was it your mother's?"

"Where's the coffee you promised me? I need it to take the Advil."

"You mustn't keep secrets from me," Paul admonished.

"Why not?"

He brushed past her to pour the coffee. It smelled delicious. She was suddenly very thirsty.

Paul set a mug in front of her. She sidled into a chair and downed the two capsules with a big gulp of coffee. Paul sat facing her, his back to the window. She pulled the laptop to her and cradled her head on its cool, black lid.

"You gave up your rights to secrets when you signed on with me. Remember?"

"No."

"Just a few short weeks ago you were willing to give me much more than your secrets for a chance to get off the tenth floor."

"That, I remember," Ladesque muttered. Her headache was subsiding, but the knowledge that had exacerbated it, was not disappearing. In fact, it was becoming more prominent. Her father and mother had both given their lives fighting to see justice for her. What hurt almost as much was that her country, Canada, the land of her birth had killed her parents, or at the very least been part of the conspiracy that left her and thousands of others bereft of their sexuality.

"What's bothering you, Ladesque?"

"A migraine," she said.

"Something you discovered in here?" he asked, tapping the computer.

"And you—you're bothering me, too."

Paul said nothing more. He looked out over the winter streetscape, staring perhaps at the Rockies—far in the distance. The natural light streaming in from the low winter sun highlighted his cheekbones and chin in the most marvellous of manner.

With each sip of warm, rich coffee, the pain in Ladesque's head subsided a bit more. Her nausea disappeared and the stiffness in her shoulders and neck evaporated. She felt very tired.

"The committee is ready to start the project," Paul eventually said. "Are you ready?"

Ladesque thought of life without the project. Her life—empty and dull and depressing. *I have no choice.* "Yes," she answered. Just then, her doorbell rang.

CHAPTER 25

"So, you're okay?" Roach asked. He stood just inside the door, shifting from one foot to the other—his eyes darting between Paul to Ladesque. "I was worried. You wouldn't answer your phone."

"I had a migraine. I'm okay now, yes."

"Should I come in?" he asked hopefully.

"Either come in or leave," Ladesque said. "One way or another, we have to close the door before we all freeze."

"Thanks." He quickly stepped in, slammed the door, and kicked off his shoes. He looked at Ladesque expectantly.

"Want a coffee?" she offered.

"Bonus!" Roach hurried past her. He had yet to make eye contact with Paul and Paul had yet to quit staring at him. Ladesque hunted in the cupboard for another cup. "Is that your parents' old Lenovo?" Roach whistled appreciatively and reached for the laptop.

"Don't touch, Roach," Ladesque said. She set his coffee in front of him and topped up Paul's and hers.

"I'll bet I could make this old baby do things you never dreamed possible. Come on, Ladesque. Let me have a look."

"The lady said hands off," Paul growled. He leaned across the table and planted his face just inches from Roach's.

Roach met his gaze. "Hands off to you, too, buddy."

Ladesque picked up the computer and carried it into her bedroom. She tossed it onto her bed and threw the duvet over it. She stood for a moment, listening for the men's voices. It was not the computer they were fighting over. She knew that. Her father had always said if you wanted two dogs to stop fighting, you ought to take away the bone. The computer and her were now both in the bedroom and the squabbling in the dinette had stopped.

The entire house was deathly quiet. Her ears hummed. She swallowed. Tiny bits of left over migraine deep in her brain began pulsing. And between her legs—

"Ladesque!" Paul shouted. "Get out here!"

She was tired. Migraines always made her tired. She wanted to curl up under the covers with the laptop and close her eyes. In her post-migraine world there would be no raging thoughts to keep her awake. Her body would relax along with her mind—every part of her being so relieved to be rid of the agony.

The feeling in her crotch intensified. Paul was so beautifully symmetric and Roach so warm and cuddly—

"Do you want us to leave?" Roach called.

"Speak for yourself, Roach," Paul said. "Ladesque, I'm not leaving. If you don't come out here, I'll come in after you." She was obviously still a bone of contention. She walked slowly up the hall to the dinette. The men did not notice her.

"Don't you dare!" Roach said. "Nobody goes in a lady's bedroom without permission. There are laws against—"

"I'm a special agent with the FBI and you're a geek from the tenth floor. Don't tell me about laws!"

"Perhaps I'm the one who'll leave," Ladesque interrupted.

They were both so delicious looking. The sun was low, burnishing their faces with a mystical gold wash—as if they were statues. In a shrine. Greek gods.

She could toss the computer to the floor and all three of them could tumble onto the bed and beneath the covers—

"Don't be silly," Paul said. His voice was so smooth and deep. Commanding. Powerful. "Sit. Drink your coffee before it cools. Roach is on his way out. Why don't you say goodbye to him and we can get on with our meeting?"

Roach stood. "I'm *not* on my way out, Mr. Special FBI Guy." One hip was lower than the other, as if he was soldier who'd been wounded in battle. A hero, shaken but still fighting. "You are the one giving her migraines. YOU! Not me. What you're asking her to do is not something you'd ask your sister to do, or your daughter. I can guarantee you that. You're using her. Just because…just because she…Just because she's a eunuch you think she's of no value. That she's dispensable. That—"

"Ho, whoa, there! What's the lady been telling you?" Paul stared accusingly at Ladesque.

"I've told him nothing!" she protested.

"Don't blame *her*," Roach hissed. "I might be only a tenth floor geek but you know I have my sources. And I know…I know you are up to no fucking good!"

"*Fucking?*" Paul chuckled. "You, a dyed-in-the-wool geek said 'fucking'? Holy shit, NOW you've got me running scared!"

"Guys!" Ladesque shouted. The men quieted and looked at her. She stepped toward them. "Paul, quit being so condescending and Roach, I don't need you to protect me. Even you thinking I do is in its own way condescending. Both of you quit spying on me. Now, clear out of here.

I need to shower and get on with my day." She also needed to see to the problem between her legs.

Paul rose. "There's little of the day left." He followed Roach to the door.

"That's perfect," Ladesque said. "I'll shower and eat and then sleep off the headache."

Paul opened the door and waved Roach out ahead of him. "I expect to see you at the office tomorrow morning," he said. He stepped out and began closing the door. "Your two weeks leeway to get your life in order was up ten days ago. My patience has expired."

"Don't do it, Ladesque!" Roach hollered. "He's just using you. You don't have to do it."

CHAPTER 26

December 11, 2035

Paul looked a lot less like a god this morning. Ladesque took a seat in his office across from his desk. Beneath the covers last night, in her mind, in the dark he'd been muscular and hard and overcome with passion. Out of control. This morning he looked pretty well like an ordinary man, a bit frazzled around the edges even.

"Before we proceed any farther with the project…" he was saying. He'd proceeded promptly and with vigour last night in her fantasy. So had Roach. The two of them together, over-powering her, arousing her against her will. Making her beg—

"…so, that's where it sits." He squeaked his chair forward and straightened. It was obviously her turn to talk.

"Why are you so mean to Roach?"

"Mean? To Roach?"

"You treat him as if he's a piece of shit."

"I treat him like he's a tenth floor geek, Ladesque. No more, no less. He's a person you definitely don't need in your life right now."

"Isn't that my decision?"

Paul wrinkled his brow. "You actually want him hanging around? Please don't tell me you have the hots for him. Maybe it was you who told him about the nature of our project?"

"I told him nothing! Now you're treating *me* in a condescending manner. I hate your arrogance!"

"Settle down. I'm just protecting you. Roach has a crush on you and that can't be encouraged."

"Why not?"

"Think about it. Think about the project, your asexuality. Roach says I'm using you. It's him who is using you. He's using you for a safe date. He sees you as a sexless doll he can practice his kisses on. He's using you to build up his courage and repertoire of experience so he can go on to establish a mature man-woman relationship with someone who's not a eunuch. You don't need that. Not now."

Throughout this whole tirade, he's not looked me in the eye once. "I'll have you know I value his friendship." *I could swear he's jealous, but why would he be if he thinks I'm a eunuch?*

"Well, please value it when I'm not around. I can't stand the man, and I use the term *'man'* loosely."

Ladesque rolled her eyes and sat back in her chair. Obviously, she'd have to let Paul and Roach sort out their relationship as she apparently wasn't going to be given any say in it.

"We need to get on with this, so please. Answer my question."

"I don't know what your question was. I wasn't listening."

"I asked you what was on your dad's computer that upset you so much."

"I'm sure you told me why you need to know that. Tell me again, I missed that part, too."

"I need to know all your secrets because our little quantum computer is going to read both your mind and your brain and anything in them is going to become part of the programming. What was on the laptop?"

"There was a conspiracy between the pharmaceutical company and the Canadian government to cover up the fact it was known the pill would produce a generation of female eunuchs before it was released."

"I can tell you right now, that's bullshit."

"No. My dad uncovered documents showing the government invested heavily in the development and research of this particular pill. And stood by it and approved it, even though studies were available showing it was trouble."

"That's not true, Ladesque. Why would the government want to produce a generation of asexual women?"

"Studies suggested asexual females would provide a stable labour force, perhaps lower the crime rate—"

"Does any of that make sense to you?"

"Perhaps they saw a lucrative market in emerging nations concerned about their birth rates. Perhaps they considered the economic benefits of a generation not prone to STDs. Perhaps they thought cultures intent on desexualizing women would buy the product to offset the demise of the burka and female genital mutilation. I don't know. I don't care. The fact is, they went ahead with the drug, distributed it, and covered up their involvement—"

"Not true. So not true."

"I can show you. My dad has it all recorded—on a computer without internet capabilities. Documents scanned in. Committee minutes. Financial reports. Research dating back to the early 1900s right up until he died."

"Listen to me!" Paul slammed his fist to his desk, making Ladesque jump. She'd not anticipated his fury. "Listen! For one thing the crash of cyberspace was an insidious thing. Hackers started to manipulate data way back when PC's first became mainstream and right on up to when Wikileaks first started to dribble. Despite the fact your dad's computer wasn't internet ready, the documents and data on it could well have been compromised before your father scanned them in. Secondly, this is a bad case of 'knowing a little bit can be a dangerous thing'. Your father was looking for one thing, and one thing alone—someone to blame for his daughter's asexuality and his wife's death. He ignored all else. He ignored important facts. Do you know who was representing the Canadian government on the research and development committee that did the clinical trials for the drug?"

"Aside from bureaucrats, the only name Dad mentioned was a Charlie H.—the man he wanted to find and make pay."

"Charlie H. was Charlotte Hexton from TPD, Canada's Therapeutic Products Directorate. It was a woman, not a man, who oversaw the clinical trials and eventually approved the drug for public use."

"Man, woman, does it matter? Dad's suspicions were right! It was a conflict of interest for the government to first fund the research and then be the ones to approve the product. How unethical is that?"

"The Canadian government did not have a history of funding commercial research such as pharmaceuticals. But do you know why they made the exception?"

"They wanted to create a sexless generation of females—"

"No! There is no proof of such a thing anywhere! And neither he, nor I, nor you, uncovered any viable reason to explain why a government, or anyone else for that matter, would want to steal a generation's libido."

"Say whatever you want. I know what Dad uncovered."

"What did you uncover, Ladesque? In your dad's data, your mom's, on the archived internet files—what reasons did you find for Phizenhessen to research and develop a new oral contraceptive?"

"They said they wanted to make a safer birth control pill. To lower the risk of cancer—"

"Exactly! That was a big concern at the start of the millennium. But concerns larger than the small incidents of increased cancer and blood clots were emerging. Infertility in women, and men, was rising. There were environmental concerns—the hormones from these pills released in the urine of women using them were showing up downstream from cities and were being blamed for anomalies in fish and other aquatic life. Some apparently permanent problems with libido seemed linked to birth control. These were the issues the government was investing in solving and that was the mandate behind the joint venture between Canada and Phizenhessen."

"And?"

"And this pill appeared to address the most serious of those problems."

"But the studies all showed a decreased libido—"

"That was a common side-effect of not only birth control pills, but other medications as well. It wasn't deemed a unique problem with this pill. And the fact it would permanently rob libido and fertility from the upcoming generation of females was not known until it happened."

"But even when it did become known, nothing was done about it. Big government gets in bed with big industry and the ordinary citizen's rights get swept under the carpet!"

"Swept under the carpet? Hardly. Protective laws were enacted, asexual rights enshrined. Both government and industry established a litany of free support systems and mounted massive education programs. When it turned out those affected, did not feel adversely affected, yes, things were sugar-coated a bit. But that was done more to dissuade lawsuits than to cover up evil intentions. There was no conspiracy."

"You're brainwashing me! I saw it...I saw it all! I saw the conspiracy, the evil intent. It's all there! I can show you! I'll bring in the computer—"

"You don't need to show me, I already—I already know the story. Unlike you, I gathered my information from multiple sources, not just from the computer of a maniacal father lost in grief and seeking revenge."

"Don't denigrate my father! He got his information from way more sources than you'd ever be able to access!"

"He bought his information, bribed his informants, threatened them—his data is tainted, Ladesque!"

"How the fuck do you know that?" She rose. With clenched fists and eyes so narrowed she could see only his face, she leaned across his desk. "You wouldn't know that if you hadn't been on Dad's computer. You lied to me—it *was* you that broke into my house."

"Ladesque! Settle down." He lowered his voice to a bass hum. "Please, sit."

She swiped her hand across his desk, sending files and papers and pens to the floor. "I can't work with someone like you!"

"It was not me or any of my people who broke into your place. Promise. Just relax. Please sit. Listen to what I am saying. Be rational. You knew from the moment you signed the contract, you would not be allowed to keep secrets from me."

"Trade secrets, you idiot! My trade secrets about computers, technology, programming...the tenth floor secrets—that's what you bought with your contract. Not my personal..." Ladesque began to weep. She sat and buried her face behind her hands. She could not stop crying.

"It's hard. I know it's hard. We so badly want to believe our parents are perfect." *And that our country won't betray us.* "And, yes, you're right. You're entitled to your personal secrets." He stopped talking and the jagged sound of her sobs filled the silence between them. She heard him squeak back his chair and retrieve his stuff she'd scattered to the floor.

When she had no more tears and her cries went silent and inward, he began to talk again. Quietly and evenly, like one might read a nursery rhyme to a child.

"Initially, Charlie Hexton was tremendously upset the project she'd brought to fruition had such disastrous results. It haunted her that an entire generation of females was robbed of their sexual identity. She was the force behind a series of Montreal experiments to try to reverse the damage. All met with limited success. Whenever they got close to finding something that wouldn't produce asexuality, the risk of cancer, blood clots, and high blood pressure increased." He stopped as if giving her time for the information to soak in.

He expects me to believe everything he's saying. "Where did you get this information?"

"I have access to any information I request, whether it be from government, industry, or the devil himself."

She looked up at him. "My mother participated in those Montreal experiments and died from cancer."

"Yes, some of drugs experimented with proved to be carcinogenic. She knew the risks when she signed on. The drugs weren't purposely laced with carcinogens as your dad claims."

Paul tossed her a box of tissues. She drew one out and wiped her cheeks and nose. "If all was aboveboard as you say, Paul, why the secrecy?"

"The government funding was kept secret to avoid the wrath of competing pharmaceutical companies. But the data from the clinical trials and the TPD approval process was all public knowledge. Before the Great Crash, you could readily have accessed Phizenhessen's 1980's and 90s research and found all you wanted to know about the development, testing and approval of the drug. Phizenhessen's claims those records were lost in the Crash were likely made to put an end to the lawsuits. If one were to look hard enough, one could probably still find the data. Costly research like that would not have been allowed to have been destroyed."

"You're wrong. My dad uncovered irrefutable evidence the government was involved in ultra-secret pharmaceutical research and clinical trials. He fell short of finding supportive data—"

"The research he was trying to chase down involved drug trials performed on pubescent juveniles affected by the Phizenhessen drug. Because children are incapable of giving informed consent and are more vulnerable to the effects of drugs than adults, it was against the law at that time to do clinical experiments on kids. That's why the trials were kept well-hidden. As unethical as the study first appears, researchers used a minimal number of girls and obtained the same type of parental consent they would have needed to perform any medical procedure on the under-aged."

"That's all lies, Paul! Lies! I remember getting that injection when I was thirteen and I don't remember it being a secret. Besides, Mom clearly states in her diary Dad knew about it."

"He was under the impression it was hormonal treatment to enhance secondary sex characteristics, not an experimental drug trial to restore libido and fertility. Therefore, when he got whiff of a secret, government-funded experiment, he overlooked the truth and began digging for something more sinister—something that did not exist."

"I don't believe you!"

"Were you told what the injection was for?"

"I-I-no I wasn't, but that doesn't mean Mom lied to Dad about it."

"From what you know about your parents, would your Dad have agreed to let you participate in an experiment like that?"

"How would I know? How—"

"In your mom's diary and in your dad's computer, what was said about your dad's feelings—"

"Stop it! Just stop it! Both mom and dad gave their lives trying to make mine better. To insinuate otherwise is to dishonour them. You have no right to do that!"

"Does this sound familiar, *'It was a drug that caused the problem in the first place, so adding more chemicals to the mix as an attempted solution is insane'?*"

Ladesque wiped her eyes and stared at him. That was an exact quotation from one of her Dad's missives on his old Lenovo. Paul stared back, unblinking. "Face the facts, Ladesque. He did not know."

"But you do."

"I know that nothing happened after the injections. The girls passed through puberty still absent of pheromones and libido." He was scratching that spot on his desk again. *He's hiding something from me.*

"What else do you know?"

"Time pulled a trick."

"Pardon?" His scratching intensified. He was soon going to wear a hole through the glossy oak finish. He was not looking at her. *He knows everything.* Paul raised his eyebrows and closed one eye as if he were winking at her, but not quite. She remembered that look. "The eunuch author lusts after the football star and the tenth floor geek offers me her body parts."

Her diaphragm froze; she could not breathe. "You knew all along," she whispered with the last of her breath. *I've been played for a fool.* Her cheeks reddened and her heart slowed.

Paul shrugged. "There are valid reasons I could not reveal what I knew."

When she'd been at her most vulnerable, when she'd suddenly and unexpectedly been overwhelmed with powerful new feelings, he'd known it. He'd touched her, caressed and kissed her as he coerced her into the Skinner's Box project. And each time she'd tried to let him know what it was doing to her, he'd shot her down.

Roach is right, he's been using me…and it's too late to do anything about it.

CHAPTER 27

"The Skinner's Box Project has its roots far in the past," Paul said as the door sucked closed behind them. They were back in the safe in the underground computer lab—the red quantum computer pulsated in the corner. She'd not wanted to hear Paul's reasons for pretending he didn't know she was a sexual being, mostly because she didn't believe he could have good reasons for treating her as he had.

"Back in the late 1930s," Paul continued, "Skinner coined the phrase *operant conditioning.* Shortly thereafter, he built the first Skinner's Box and mankind came to realize behaviour could be measured."

But suppose he does have a good reason?

"How long does it take rats to learn to push a lever to receive food? To avoid an electric shock? To get to a female in heat?"

He was treating her no differently than before they'd laid their secrets bare that afternoon in his office. He still spoke warmly to her, smiled when he saw her, sometimes briefly laid his hand upon her shoulder. Perhaps her sexuality was irrelevant to him.

Ladesque sighed. "Because of Skinner," she said, "human behaviour became something that could be studied and understood. Predicted." *As if!*

"Correct. And we've now—"

"What are your reasons?"

"Pardon?"

"The reasons for your behavior. Why did you pretend you thought I was asexual?"

"Why did you pretend you were?"

"I-I-I didn't. Not really. I didn't know what was happening. I tried to find out but no one—"

"I gave you openings several times and all but outright asked you. To me it seemed obvious you didn't want to share that with me. I couldn't argue with that. It was, in fact, none of my business."

"Your dishonesty is *my* fault?"

"Why do you think it was up to me to comment on your sexuality?"

"Normally I wouldn't expect anyone to comment on my sexuality, except you seemed to repeatedly comment on my asexuality, so how fair is that?"

"I didn't repeatedly—"

"You said I was chosen for this project because I'm asexual—worthless, expendable, disposable—"

"I said no such thing!"

"You might as well have."

"But I didn't."

"You said I was asexual and then proceeded to treat me as if I was sexual. And then just walked away…as if our encounters meant nothing. As if I was nothing!"

"I don't recall you protesting any of our encounters."

"It's not the—the encounters I'm angry about. It's the walking away afterwards."

"But you refused to admit your sexuality to me. A man can only go so far without reciprocity before it becomes assault. What would you rather I have done?"

"NOTHING! I'd rather you had done nothing. You shouldn't have touched me! Just don't touch me. Leave me alone. Open the safe, now please, and let me out. I need to get out of here. I need OUT, NOW!"

"You can't leave." He wrapped his arm around her waist and led her to the steno chair waiting by the computer. His arm was warm; his grip was strong.

"I have to leave."

"You can't. We have a schedule to keep. Deadlines to meet. Many are depending on us to do our part so they can do theirs. The team needs you, right here and now, Ladesque. Here and now!" He pushed her into the chair and then knelt in front of her.

"Nothing has changed between us. Except now you know that I know you're not a eunuch."

"But I'm furious with you—that changes everything. A lot!

"Deal with it and move on."

"Our whole relationship over the past three months was based on a lie. How can I move on when the past is such a mess?"

Paul rose and threw his hands up in exasperation. "What do you want me to say? What do you want me to do? You lied, I lied. But the past wasn't all that bad, was it?" He bent over and peered into her eyes. "Was it?"

Oh, Lord. He's going to kiss me. "Most of it was okay."

"Just 'okay'?" He pulled her to her feet, his eyes on hers, his hands on her back sliding down to her butt, his lips brushing hers. She wrapped her arms around his neck and sought his tongue with hers. "Easy, girl," he said gently pulling away. "You can bet your bottom dollar there's a hundred security cams in here. As I was saying…" He winked at her before turning away, a true wink this time. "With our new invention, we can do for intelligence what Skinner did for behaviour—take it out of philosophy and into the science lab. Although psychologists for decades had used tests to measure intelligence, nothing was available to define or predict it. This became abundantly clear when people began talking about artificial intelligence, robotic intelligence, computer intelligence. Without a proper definition, it could not be electronically reproduced."

She licked her lips, seeking his sweet taste, and sank back into the chair. "What's the nature of our new invention?"

"It was brought about by tackling the chemistry behind the working of intelligent. The biology. The structure of the brain. The activity. The processes. With the help of another great invention that could read the chemical process of a brain's activities and digitize it, much as MRI's and CT Scans once did with electronic and magnetic signals, we were able to produce mathematical equations explaining the nature of intelligence."

"We? Who's this 'we' that discovered how to digitize intelligence?"

"Nobody could digitize intelligence, until now. A fellow by the name of Marco Rochester invented the equations but we needed a quantum computer to complete that final step of digitizing it all. We now have one."

"Why do you need me if you have Marco's equations and your computer?"

"You are the constant."

"Pardon?"

"Einstein's great equation E equals MC squared told the world energy and matter were equivalent, provided you stuck in a constant squared. The constant being the speed of light. Marco's equation tells us intelligence is equivalent to electron behaviour times a constant squared. The constant is the chemical processes of the brain. We need to scan your brain's chemistry into the computer. We need to digitize it.

"Why my brain?"

"It's close to what we want our computer to have. A high IQ. Flexible reasoning. Emotional stability."

"Asexuality?"

"We'll have to pass on that, won't we?" Paul said with a grin.

"The dangers?"

"You will be more than just scanned. You will be merging with the quanta in the computer. You will be directing them, correcting them. Braking them. You will be instilling in them the ability to go beyond your brain power. They will become self-sufficient, self-repairing, self-growing. We're not sure what effect this merging will have on you, either physically or psychologically. You may not come back to us. You may become the computer, its feeder system. As it links to you, you may become inexorably linked to it. Be drawn in. You may not be able to come back. Or, attracted to the knowledge it creates, you may not be willing to."

"I see."

"Nobody thinks that likely. During the time of the first atomic bomb, scientists worried that in setting it off they might initiate a chain reaction that would see all atoms in the entire universe explode. They thought it unlikely and took the risk. Consider this experiment equivalent."

If I were to link the quantum computer to my scrubbed files, would it be able to uncover the truth about Canada and Phizenhessen Pharmaceuticals or is the truth about my parents' deaths and my asexuality destined to be hidden forever beneath the rubble of the Great Crash?

CHAPTER 28

"Roach, what are you doing here?" Ladesque asked wearily. He was on her front step, incessantly ringing her bell. Her robot lady announcer had been driven to silence by his persistence and Ladesque had been forced to manually open the door to him. Roach pushed past her and kicked off his shoes. Paul was very close to being exactly right when he said she did not need Roach in her life right now.

"I've come here to tell you not to do it," he said bluntly.

"Not to do what?"

"Skinner's Box. Don't do it."

"How the hell do you know about Skinner's Box?" Ladesque said.

"I know all about everything." Roach strode past her to the kitchen. Ladesque slammed the door and marched in after him. He pointed to her dad's laptop that lay closed on the counter. "Including what's in there. Paul's using you, Ladesque. It isn't fair and it isn't legal."

"Roach, I know you mean well, but you are not helping anything. Paul already suspects I'm leaking info to you on the project—"

"That's not at all he's suspicious about. He's lies, that man. Lies and deceit."

"You're not making sense, Roach!"

"Ladesque, I fudged your lab results to prove you were sexual so the committee would reconsider using you in the experiment. Paul changed them back—"

"You fudged my lab results? What do you mean, you fudged my lab results?"

"Those random medical tests ordered in the spring were actually not random and not ordered by Global. They were requested by the FBI—for you only. I paid off someone in the lab, a data entry clerk, just gave her a little something and she added a few numbers in front of the zero. The test results sent to the committee showed you were producing pheromones except Paul intercepted them and changed it back to zero—"

"The lab results showed zero?"

"Of course. You're a eunuch."

"No, Roach. Listen. Did you see the lab results or are you assuming they said zero?"

"It doesn't take a genius to know without looking that a eunuch's pheromones are zero."

"I see," Ladesque said. "You didn't actually see the results."

"I didn't have to."

Ladesque closed her eyes and shook her head. "I hope the hell you didn't pay that clerk more than a week's wages," she muttered.

"What did you say?"

"Nothing. Nothing at all. I appreciated your concern, Roach. Really I do, but—"

"Ladesque, I know about the project. Everything about the project. I've been in on it for a couple of years. I know all about Skinner's Box."

"What are you telling me? You've been working with the FBI for a couple of years?"

"Well…sort of. Yeah."

"And yet you were willing to take my twenty dollar bet and the money of the other tenth floor geeks?"

"Sure. Well, I had no choice. It's all top secret. I couldn't very well tell anyone what I was doing. Even Talon and his fish didn't know. It was an after-hours, weekend-type of thing. Voluntary, sort of. Except I got paid. I wasn't physically there with them. Just doing calculations."

"Does Paul know?"

"If he didn't before, I'm sure he does now. Look, Ladesque." He laid his palm on the laptop and stared into her eyes. "If you don't want what happened to your mom and dad to happen to you, get out. Now. While you're still alive."

"Paul's not intending on killing me! You know too little about the project. I know the risks. I've been apprised—"

"No you don't and you haven't—"

"A little knowledge is a dangerous thing. You may have worked on the periphery of the project, Roach. But you don't know—"

"I know. I know it all. I know what happened to the lab rats and the chimps. I know—"

"Lab rats and chimps?"

"The ones who went before you, Ladesque. The ones whose brains were sucked into the machine…"

"Oh, for Christ's sake! No one's brains are going to be sucked into anything! This is non-invasive, Roach. The technology only reads the brain chemistry. It doesn't suck anything!"

"At the beginning that's how it is. But an hour in and that computer will have everything it ever needs from you. It will be done with acquiring knowledge. It will be creating knowledge. Altering knowledge. Doing whatever the hell it wants to the original source of that knowledge—to its creator—you, Ladesque. You!"

"I'll be very careful to program it to be kind and respectful of its creators. If it doesn't listen, one just has to unplug it."

"Perhaps not. Perhaps it will figure out how to operate off chemistry instead of electricity. Perhaps it will find the chemistry it needs in your brain. Your non-invasive technology does have a communication loop—"

"Communication is the key word. This loop allows the computer and me to communicate. It does NOT allow the computer to enter my brain and take over my synapses—"

"How do you know that? How do you know what something a million, billion, trillion times more intelligent than you will be able to do with that loop? You don't know. Nobody knows. Nobody."

"What happened to the rats and chimps?"

"Amazing things, Ladesque. The quanta uncovered endless chatter in their brains, not the base survival instincts scientists expected of such lowly creatures. Both the rats and chimps communicate about things other than food, shelter and sex. The quantum computer deciphered their conversations as easily as if they were a code. These creatures were speaking—never mind."

"Speaking?"

"The computer translated their conversations into rhythms and colours. Some scientists said music, others poetry. Many mentioned—never mind."

"Mentioned what?

"*Close Encounters,* the movie. Did you ever see that old movie about—"

"Yes, I saw it. The aliens first communicated with humans via music and lights. And this is all exceptionally interesting, but how does it affect me, Roach? What is it about the rats and chimps that frightens you?"

"The longer the animals were attached to Skinner's Box, the more intelligible their conversations became."

"Skinner's Box got better at deciphering it as time went on, just as it's supposed to."

"The other theory is that the mice got better at conversing as time went on."

"You think Skinner's Box was teaching the rats? Increasing their intelligence? Feeding them info?"

"I don't know," Roach said. "The experiments had to end because the computer hit its programmed limits. But..."

"The animals survived? All of them? Did they appear super intelligent afterwards?"

"They survived. Physically they seemed fine. Their intelligence was hard to test, given that unlike Skinner's Box, scientists can't understand mouse talk. However, they did do the typical Skinner's Box trials—the old Skinner's Box, the lever and maze tests."

"And?"

"The raw data results were never released. The summary report said there was a slight to insignificant increase in their ability to learn. However, the researchers also pointed out that running intelligent creatures through mazes might not be an accurate way to measure their IQ."

"Why does the fact I may come back more intelligent seem threatening to you?"

"If Skinner's Box is capable of intruding into the basic brains of rats, how the hell do we know what it will do if it gets into a human brain?"

"I know I face risks, but they're low. It's unlikely anything untoward will happen—"

"But the results are catastrophic if they do."

"History is full of examples of scientists overlooking such slim possibilities. The particle accelerator under the Franco-Swiss border could have produced black holes able to swallow the earth. The Eagle may have sunk out of sight into the dusty surface of the moon, never allowing Neil Armstrong to take a small step—"

"You're right, but this is...this is *you* at risk. You. You whom the committee deemed disposal and fit for the part. You're not disposable, Ladesque. Your mother and father both died because they understood your importance to the world. I'm taking up that torch."

"Why?"

He blushed and stammered and then reached for her hand. "Forgive me. I know this is so wrong and totally illegal. But I can't help it. I can't..." Tears welled in his eyes. "I love you."

CHAPTER 29

Ladesque had been bombarded with information over the past four weeks, sopping up all the knowledge those in the know wanted imparted to Skinner's Box. And her sex drive had vanished. She had no swelling down below. No fantasies. No urges. It was gone. Roach came over one night. Drank a beer, shook her hand and left. Her pheromones had cut out again. She knew beyond a doubt.

"We need to talk about ASB," Paul said. He still looked at her as if she was desirable.

"ASB?"

"After Skinner's Box. We'd like you to stay with the project, Ladesque. Set up protocols for handling the information the computer generates, controlling access to it. Analyzing applications, approving networks. It will be a big job. Not one you can do by yourself, but one you would oversee, along with the committee of course."

"Do I have a choice?" *As if I wouldn't jump at the chance!*

"The committee has said all along your contractual obligations to the project would end once you completed the biological programming. In their minds, compelling you to keep with the project after taking on the tremendous risks associated with programming would not be reasonable."

"How secure would it be though, to let me go at that point?"

"It depends on where you were to go," Paul said. "If you were to head upstairs to the office of the Executive Director of Computer Technology, I foresee no threat to security."

"I'll think about it."

"I'll tell the committee you've agreed."

"I—"

"I know you well enough to know Skinner's Box is your baby and you'll never let it go."

"You are assuming I'm going to come out fine on the other side. What if I return a bumbling idiot? What kind of Computer Director would I be then?"

"I would not let you do this if I believed anything like that were possible."

"What's it going to be like to connect to the computer, Paul? What has it already been programmed to do?"

"It will pick up bits of knowledge from your chemistry, analyze it, and check back with you, asking you to correct any errors in its understanding. It will go from there to simple things like mathematical formulas and results. Perhaps confirming the value of pi. And carrying on to the English language. To emotional responses. To behaviour. You must help it to grow and understand. It must be able to make self-corrections after you withdraw. You must instil in it logic. The basics of scientific thought and reasoning. The necessity of predicting and explaining."

"That's sounds like a lot to do."

"Remember, you'll have the power of a quantum computer helping you. By all estimates, it will be a cake walk. There's another thing you can do, but it's not compulsory." He paused and scraped at the floor with his shoe. "You can ask it to help you reverse your asexuality. It's up to you. If it turns out to be a complicated procedure, painful, dangerous, beyond our physicians' abilities, it might not be worth it to you. Especially since normal menopausal changes will be rendering you, Tracy Spence and a dozen other 'children of the pill' sexless within a decade or so with or without the reversal. You decide."

"Menopausal women aren't 'sexless'. Infertile, perhaps, but still fully capable of arousal and orgasm."

"In a reduced capacity," Paul had said flippantly.

"I want Roach with me when I'm hooked up."

"Why?"

He said he'd rip the thing off my head if there was any inkling of a problem—something I'm pretty sure you wouldn't do.

"He knows how to keep me relaxed."

"You're lying."

"I get to keep personal secrets, remember?"

"I'll ask the committee and the technical staff if we can honour that request."

CHAPTER 30

She hadn't yet decided. Sex was delicious but over-powering. Being sexual was being a slave to her body. However, you couldn't say sex was anymore more enslaving that hunger or thirst. She was a physical being, driven by physical needs. Always had been, always would be. And sex was just another physical need. Albeit, a need tied more closely to emotional needs than most—

"One more thing before we start," Paul said. She'd thought they were on the way to the lab, but he put a hand on her elbow and directed her toward the exit. Outside the glass doors, the January sun was glinting off snow banks higher than her head. "Skinner's Box is an international project," Paul continued. "Our major partner has requested an audience with you."

He opened the door for her and hustled her across the street into the wintery park. The bright sun had a bit of warmth. However, it was low and in her eyes—its dazzle bleaching out her view of what lay ahead. If she'd known she'd be hiking outdoors, she'd have put on her sunglasses and her coat. She shivered and wrapped her sweater around her tighter.

"There's a reason I didn't let you into the tenth floor vault when you first asked," Paul said. "I didn't want you to uncover the link between the Canadian government and the Phizenhessen fiasco." He'd slipped on reflective sunshades, making it impossible to tell where he was looking. She assumed he was scanning her face for her reaction.

"There was information about that on the 2010 internet?"

"If you'd known what to look for, you may have found enough data to spark your suspicions. You are, after all, notoriously able to uncover patterns in raw data."

"Why didn't you want me to know about the Canadian government's link to Phizenhessen?"

Paul came to a halt and removed his sunglasses. "Ladesque, this is Jack Steward from the Canadian Embassy, representing our major partner in the Skinner's Box project."

Ladesque raised her hand to shade her eyes. The man before her was staid and proper, in a dark suit, his eyes hid behind even darker glasses.

He flashed an ID card and extended his hand. "Pleased to finally meet you, Sally."

He knows my real name?

Ladesque nervously looked over her shoulder at Paul's retreating back. *Canada is his partner? Was all his chatter about the virtuosity of the Canada-Phizenhessen partnership just bullshit to ensure I'd be willing to work with Canada to complete this project?*

"Are you frightened of *me* or your pending date with the computer?" Jack asked.

Paul disappeared into the building. If it wasn't Paul who'd broken into her place, chances were high it had been his partner. The Canadian government had lots of reasons to find out what she knew before letting her participate. She turned to Jack. He still had his hand extended. "I guess that depends on why you are here." In deference to protocol she finally accepted his handshake, which was surprisingly warm and gentle, unlike the firm, frozen grip she offered him.

"Relax. I know about your research into your parents' deaths. My presence here has nothing to do with those circumstances or the circumstances surrounding asexuality."

"I have a hard time believing what you're saying, knowing your government authorized someone to break into my house."

"Was anything taken?"

"No, but—"

"Then, it wasn't my government—we would have got what we went looking for."

"What would you have been looking for?"

"It's all over now, Ladesque. Let it go."

"I need the truth." *Are you going to prevent me from getting that?*

"The truth is your mother died from experimental drugs she willingly took but that unfortunately a decade later proved carcinogenic. Your father died an accidental death at the hands of a drunk driver. You were the victim of faulty research based on good intentions. It's now over. You are going to find the knowledge needed to reverse the effects. It's over and you have won; the Canadian government rejoices with you."

"That's what this meeting is about?"

"On behalf of Canada, as a partner in the Skinner's Box project, I want to wish you well and thank you for accepting the personal danger associated with this project. You remind me of Canada's early explorers and pioneers who, despite facing many dangers, both known and unknown, were driven to explore, to find new worlds, to learn new things. You are even more heroic than them, however. Let's sit." He waved her to a concrete park bench that looked cold even though it was bathed in sunlight.

She walked toward it, keeping Jack in her line of sight. She trusted no one.

"Sit there," he requested, pointing to the far end of the bench. She obliged and he sank onto the end that was against a mountain ash tree. "I need the seclusion." He looked down at his hands and rubbed a thumb over his left sleeve. Ladesque was startled to see the fabric change beneath his touch from a dark serge to a touch screen, complete with a digital keyboard.

"This would be so much more impressive," he said, "if we had the internet up and running. As it is, I'm connected to the Prime Minister's office should you wish to consult with her directly."

He quit talking and began fingering the buttons. Her amazement left her speechless.

A small smile lifted Jack's lips as he stared at the text on the screen. "Prime Minister Tschan sends her greetings and appreciation. He tilted his arm as if to show her what was written. "You're on camera, smile," he said. "She'd love to see your face light up; it would soothe her fears about your future."

She pointed to his sleeve. "How can you do that?"

"Do what? The fabric? The LiveCam? Or Texting?"

"How can you communicate like this, wirelessly, without…?"

"We've got it covered," Jack said. He tapped a few times on his sleeve, drew his hand over the screen and it morphed back into the dark of his jacket. "I think we have about nine communication satellites of our own, programmed specifically and solely for the use of the Canadian government. Totally different technology than was available before the Great Crash. Technology compatible with Skinner's Box."

"Do the Americans know about these satellites?"

Jack shrugged. "We like to think not, but we're wise enough not to bet on it." He paused and then patted his sleeve. "However, they *do* know about the fabric. It was a joint effort."

"The fabric?"

"With flexible threads able to carry electronic signals woven right into the material. Throw in some water-proofing and we have magic."

"I see. That explains why I never uncovered the security camera in my office. It's probably embedded in the Persian rug hanging on the wall."

"No more lost SmartPhones, Google at your fingertips. Instantaneous communication around the world…if we ever get the internet up and running. That's not why I'm here, though. Obviously. Although I do want to point out some very useful results of your pending date with Skinner's Box."

"How much do you know about Skinner's Box?"

"Secrets are scarce when you share the same bedroom."

"Bedroom?"

He sucked in a quick breath. "My apologies. Not a good analogy, considering your circumstances. This entire project," he said waiving toward the compound that housed the textile plant and underground tunnels to the lab, "is a joint endeavour between the Canadian and American governments. The seeds for cooperation were sown with our very successful and useful Canadarm during the space station heydays as well as our close-knit economies and mutual desire to come out in front following the Great Crash. Few know it, but Canada had its own booming cyber-technology before things collapsed, coupled with a few close relationships with nations on the cusp of high-tech."

"China?"

"Perhaps. The point is, now it's just the two of us, the U.S. and Canada, collaborating on textiles and quanta and you're at the center of it all."

"The tenth floor, I mean Global Construction—a mutual project as well?" Jack shrugged. "You're not going to tell me your secrets?" Ladesque asked.

"How many of yours are you willing to share?" She knew from the intense way he looked at her, with raised brows, that he was asking more than a simple question.

"None," she said, quickly. Selling out her workmates to the very government that killed her parents, rated nowhere on her bucket list. "If you're asking me to be a spy, the answer is no." Besides, espionage was dangerous and she already faced enough danger with Skinner's Box.

"That's not a problem. I realize it is not your personal desire for adventure that's prompting your participation in programming the quantum computer. Your mission will see few rewards accrued to you, but the world will bask in the results of your journey. Once again, everyone will have instant communications around the globe, totally secure systems to share information, a boundless ability to store data, continuous creation of new knowledge. Because you've agreed to be our constant, human intelligence will be more than doubled, more than squared. It will be infinite in amount and complexity."

He paused and rubbed his knee. A calculator appeared in the fabric. "Heat sensitive," he said. As he had no need for mathematical assistance at the moment, she had the distinct feeling he was working hard to impress her. It was unsettling to realize how well he was succeeding.

"Having said all that," he finally continued. "It's my duty to confirm you truly are participating on your own free will. Canada cannot allow one of its most valued citizens to be coerced into such a dangerous operation."

"I'm aware of all dangers. I've agreed to do it."

"Good. That's good." He pulled an envelope from his pocket. It sported the embossed gold seal of Parliament. "A letter of thanks from Prime Minister Tschan," he said. She nodded and slipped the envelope into her jacket pocket. "She'd be honoured if you were to read it before you go under, so to speak."

"I understand." Ladesque pulled it out, wondering if he intended to flick on his LiveCam again and flash the Prime Minister a picture of her reading the congratulatory letter.

Jack clasped her hand. "Later would be fine," he said. "Once you're back inside."

CHAPTER 31

As Paul led her down the ramp and through the tunnels toward the quantum computer, she pulled out the Prime Minister's letter. It was a lengthy, personal, handwritten note covering two entire pages of official stationery. But it was more than that, interspersed with the congratulations, thanks, and condolences and apologies over her parents' deaths, were tiny marks, tiny Pitman slashes, dashes, and circles designed to look like a security watermark.

One country must not be the sole possessor of such power. Program 'sober second thought.' Ladesque understood the historic reference. 'A place for sober second' was how Canada's first Prime Minster, Sir John A. Macdonald, had described the Canadian senate, mandated to review all legislation before it became law.

It was not a veto over U.S. control Canada wanted, but rather a built-in governor that could not be easily over-ridden by anyone. No one person or nation was to have unbridled accesses to the incredible knowledge the computer would be accumulating, creating, and possessing and restrictions would be placed on the computer itself.

Here's what you must do and what we'll do to make that happen. As she perused the complicated instructions, it struck her how versatile Pitman Shorthand was—it easily accommodated the high-tech terminology, even words and phrases that hadn't existed when Pitman was invented.

She memorized the instructions and tucked the envelope back in her pocket. She'd once told Paul she wanted to unleash the quantum computer on the world. She'd not understood then, the infinite potential of Skinner's Box, nor the plethora of potent technologies waiting to interlink with its intelligence.

The letter increased her confidence in her country. Canada had been known internationally as a peace keeper for almost a century; it obviously didn't take that role lightly. Perhaps it was as Paul said about her parents' death and her dilemma—no one, no company, no government had purposely harmed anybody. Perhaps it was time to let it all go.

Paul opened the lab. Ladesque followed him in and smiled to see Roach was there, grinning nervously at her.

"I'll be in the observation room," Paul said. "We want as little distraction in here as possible." He glared at Roach as he said it before slipping out the side door.

"Who's all watching?" she asked Roach, nodding to the glass wall to her left, which was obviously a giant one-way mirror.

"Just the committee."

Ladesque lay down on what looked like the exam table in a doctor's office, except no paper sheet covered the faux leather. The technician began taping wires to her head. "The secret committee I never had the privilege of meeting. I often wondered if it really existed or was just another of Paul's lies."

"The best liars are those who often tell the truth," Roach said. He leaned forward and whispered, "I'm willing to risk my life to stop the programming, so promise me no matter how involved you become in the process of information transference and creation you will respond to me when I ask you to."

"Promise," she said with a nod, which caused the technician to curse.

"Shit!" The woman bent to pick up a lead that had dropped to the floor. "Lay still and close your eyes!"

"Perhaps, don't respond with a nod," Roach suggested with a half-smile. "Once they start the process they won't let me talk to you because auditory stimuli will affect your brain chemistry too much. I can hold your hand, that's all, and it must be right from the start and constantly so it doesn't change anything." The technician left to fiddle with some dials in the corner and Roach wrapped both her hands in his.

She felt his fingers playing against her palm. Once. Twice. Flitting. Pausing. At first she thought it was nervous fidgeting, but then she picked up a pattern—fingertips, knuckles. It seemed he was trying to send her a message. His subtle movements reminded her of a scene she would never forget in Helen Keller's autobiography. The nanny signed 'water' into Helen's palm and suddenly she realized there were words for things. With words, her desolate isolation vanished.

Slowly, carefully Roach's fingers moved. She struggled to visualize the movements. *Is he forming letters? Was that an 'A'?* He repeated the series of strokes. Suddenly, it became clear. "Do you know American Sign Language?" Roach was asking.

She gasped and her eyes flew open. How often had she signed uncomplimentary things about him, in front of him, in the office? Had he seen what she'd said? What about the times she talked to herself? *My God! What all has he overheard? What all have I said while within his sight?*

"Are you all right? Did that hurt?" the technician asked.

"I'm fine. I was just thinking of…something. I'll try to relax." Roach's fingers had quit moving. *Whether or not he's seen me sign, there's no use denying my ability to do so now.* She shifted position slightly, hoping her movement would conceal her response as she signed, yes.

"Answer yes or no to all my questions so I know you're safe," he silently continued. "Flexed thumb for yes, curled pinkie, no."

"We're ready," the tech said.

Ladesque looked up at Roach. Lines of worry wrinkled his face. "It's okay," she said, giving him a big grin. "I'm going to be okay."

"I'll dim the lights to reduce stimuli," the tech said. "No more talking. As well, I suggest you close your eyes. Again. And keep them closed this time."

"Your dad's laptop," Roach signed. "There was a faulty connection. I fixed it." He loosely wrapped her hand in both of his, giving her the room and privacy to sign back.

"When?"

"The day I broke into your apartment."

Her eyes almost shot open, but she concentrated on her breathing until her heart slowed. "You?" she finally signed.

"I needed something to stop the project—or at least stop the committee from choosing you."

"Did you find anything?"

"Your dad's Lenovo. It wasn't enough."

At first she felt nothing except Roach's hands tapping out the messages. But faintly at first and then more clearly, she became aware her chemistry was being read, digitized. It was an odd sensation, similar to how she felt when she could see inside her eye while the optometrist was examining it with the light.

"I shared the Lenovo info with Paul," Roach signed.

"You did what?" she shouted out loud, sitting up. Wires tugged at her head, buzzers screamed and bells rang.

The technician came running. "What's wrong?" she asked, her fingers reaching to disconnect the leads from Ladesque scalp.

"Ladesque, shush!" Roach cast a nervous glance over his shoulder and then turned to the technician. "It's okay," he assured her as he gently pried her fingers from the wires. "She's just very nervous."

"Are you telling me that not only did you break into my house, snoop through my stuff and read my dad's computer, but then went and shared that with Paul?"

"Ssshhhh! Lay down." Roach laid a hand on each of her shoulders and pressed her toward her pillow. "I had to."

"Is it not enough this damned computer gets to read my innermost thoughts? You feel you have a right to invade my privacy, too?" Ladesque ripped his hands from her shoulder and threw her feet over the side of the bed. "You, the friend I trusted most! What the hell is it about top secret projects that makes everyone think they are entitled to act like unethical asses? Why does everyone think I have no rights just because I agreed to do this? What the hell—"

"What the hell's going on here?" The door flew open and Paul was advancing toward them.

"I think we should stop," the technician said meekly. "I should—"

"I knew I shouldn't have allowed the prick in here." Paul pointed at Roach. "Out!"

"No way!" Ladesque shouted. She began ripping the wires from her head, the sting of the sticky tape catching at her curls went unnoticed. "He goes nowhere. I need to talk to him." The technician scrambled to gather the wires as Ladesque threw the last of them behind her and hopped off the table. She lunged at Roach but he sidled behind a chair out of reach.

Paul grabbed her elbow. "You're not talking to him or anyone else." He was gritting his teeth so hard, his molars squeaked between words. "Countless man-hours have been invested in this billion dollar project and you, my dear, are going to lie down on that table." He began pushing her backwards. "As you are required to do under your contract…"

She heard little else of what Paul said once she saw Roach off to the side subtly signing to her. Not wanting Paul to notice, she gave in and let him guide her backwards to the table.

"I had to." Roach was pleading with his eyes for forgiveness. "Paul had plans for you after the break-in. He believed you weren't safe. I let him know I was the intruder so he wouldn't…" Paul moved between her and Roach and the sentence remained unfinished.

"Lie down!" Paul ordered. He turned to the technician. "How badly affected are we from all this?"

"I was still getting baseline readings, nothing was feeding through yet. The effect is negligible. We can start over." She waved the wires. "Please, all of you go for a coffee or something while I re-set. I need a good half hour."

Ladesque started to rise, but Paul roughly shoved her back down. "You stay until I say otherwise." He turned to Roach. "Out! Now! GO!"

Roach squared his shoulders and came out from behind the chair. "I'm staying with Ladesque. We have a deal, Paul." To Ladesque he signed, *I traded your dad's data for the chance to be with you here. It was worth it.*

Feeling no need for privacy, she answered aloud. "That should've been *my* decision, not yours!"

Paul stepped toward Roach, his face red with rage. "You," he said, jabbing his finger in Roach's face, "will do as I say. Out!"

"No. We have a deal—"

"Once a contract is breached, it is null and void and you breached ours by talking to Ladesque while she was on the table. The deal's dead and I'm ordering you out of here."

"Please, could you ALL leave?" the technician asked quietly.

"I'd love to," Ladesque said, without moving a muscle. "If only I were allowed to."

Paul looked from the technician, to Ladesque, to Roach and then beckoned Roach and Ladesque to follow and headed for the door. "We'll discuss this in the other room."

As she walked to the door, Ladesque's anger wound tighter and tighter. As soon as her feet hit the hallway, she exploded. "Why is it that you both think you can make better decisions for me than I can make for myself?" She ran to keep up with Paul's stride as he headed to the meeting room. "Do I strike you as incapable of looking after myself? Do you—"

"You kick me out of that room, Paul," Roach interrupted, "and you'll find out who wields the ultimate power around here. I'll give you a clue—it's not those with the biggest desk or fanciest title—it's those who control the technology!"

"Don't you threaten me." Paul's voice quavered as a bass guitar did after having been slowly strummed—deep and menacing, rippling into eternity. It frightened Ladesque but Roach seemed unmoved.

Roach stepped in front of Paul and stopped dead. "Watch me." He stuck out his chin. "Just watch me, Special FBI Guy."

Paul threw up his hands and looked to the heavens. "Dear Lord, please help me." He looked at Ladesque and then Roach. "Does no one around here have an ounce of maturity? I have a billion dollar project at risk and two blubbering idiots intent on screwing it up for what reasons? What the hell reasons do either of you have for this tirade? Can you not step outside your petty little selves for two hours while we get this programming done? Two hours, people. For two hours think of the world instead of yourselves. Consider what is at stake—and I don't just mean the money and time invested. Think of all the benefits we won't have if we don't proceed. Think of the social, environmental and medical benefits. Communications. Space travel. Hell, maybe even time travel. Then, take a minute to consider what might happen if we don't do this and someone beats us to it. If you've never contemplated Armageddon, I suggest you contemplate it now."

Roach dropped his gaze and shuffled awkwardly.

Paul turned to Ladesque. "Tell me again what it is that's bothering you?"

Thoughts about Phizenhessen and asexuality flashed through her mind amidst images of solving world hunger and establishing world peace. "I-I-" Some geek in a basement somewhere programming a super computer to enslave the world and make him the master. "I'm sorry. It's okay."

"And you?" Paul said, directing his attention to Roach. "Still contemplating sabotaging the program?"

"I'm staying in that room with Ladesque."

"I'll make you a new deal. I let you hold Ladesque's hand and you won't sabotage a single technical thing?"

"Sounds fine by me," Roach mumbled.

Ladesque was sure she saw Paul roll his eyes as he shepherded them back to the lab.

CHAPTER 32

Somewhere, inside, she felt the computer communicating. *"If three plus two is five, five minus two is three?"*

She thought 'yes' and that seemed to be all that was needed.

"If tectonic plates move at the rate of six centimeters per annum..."

The questions got quicker, tougher, and soon were beyond her. She watched, fascinated. Knowledge was replicating, quadruplicating, solving, evolving. More and more the computer questioned itself, rather than her. The conversations pinged back and forth. Some echoed, some repeated. Some lagged a bit behind. The voices multiplied, much as conversations at parties did as more and more guests arrived. Soon Ladesque was no longer a participant, simply an observer. It was time now, before it was all over, to program sober second thought.

However, the moment she intruded in the computer's conversation, it protested, bucked. Stalled. She searched back through the thick layers of data for the basic programming done before the chemical equations began. She panicked for a moment when it seemed the simple programming was lost. But then she found it, and flagged it, and made a permanent shortcut to it. Humans might not be able to control the data, but they had to always be able to control the machine producing it. Always.

She instructed the computer to keep pursuing knowledge while she tweaked the operating system. There was a hesitation. "Keep going," she encouraged. She struggled through the extensive initial coding, until she found the right place to build in the controls and set the new parameters. She struggled to define illicit tasks and then programmed the computer to prevent the completion of such projects. She doubled that up with a well-disguised firewall. If the controls in the initial code were circumvented, the computer was programmed to provide inaccurate information, if need be, to foil illegal activity. Basically, she programmed an ability to lie.

"Are you there?" Roach signed.

Technicians would undoubtedly be called in to troubleshoot if the computer responded in ways other than expected so she wove the secret deeper and deeper—out of sight. The techies would look for incompatible files or hardware, rogue programming codes, physical malfunctions. Electronic interference. Hackers. They'd pour over debriefing notes, and user manuals, and ask Skinner's Box to fix itself. She had to make sure it wouldn't.

Once a questionable activity began, sober second thought was initiated and Skinner's Box would let its masters know it could not proceed. She programmed in the complex formula that would re-start Skinner's Box, an extensive process that would require the input and approval of at least two nations.

"Are you all right?" Roach asked. She flexed her thumb.

She had a panoramic view of the potential, the expanding knowledge base, the calculations. Now that she'd successfully set limits on the computer's human masters, she must program limits to Skinner's Box itself. She somehow had to digitize the concept of morality in very basic form. She couldn't just program in her morality, no matter how generic it was, because the new knowledge that was sure to gush forth from Skinner's Box would undoubtedly alter mankind's understanding and definition of morality. She struggled with defining concepts such as, *the end doesn't always justifying the means,* and *the majority must respect the rights of the minority.* She tried to explain how to discern the rights of an individual versus the rights of the species. She wondered if *Maslow's Hierarchy of Needs,* starting with food, clothing, and shelter and ending with self-actualization, could help the computer decide the appropriateness of progress, processes, inventions and possibilities.

Skinner's Box needed a strong sense of morality, not only to ensure its output was appropriate but also so it could recognize if it was being abused.

Amazingly, all her ideas fell through cyberspace like flour through a sifter, coming out pure and soft and ready to blend on the other side. Skinner's Box began creating for itself the ability to limit its actions to those that were beneficial. She could never have done such complicated programming herself, but she was experiencing firsthand the power of a working quantum computer. Things started going faster, falling into place, merging, melding.

Amazed, she watched. It was as if knowledge had become a breathing, moving, living plasma.

It seemed like mere moments before her programming was done. She stepped back for a broader view. The system was smooth, expanding outward at a tremendous speed like a quantum scale imitation of the Big Bang.

She took a tentative step back toward consciousness on the table in the lab. Nothing was in her way, she felt no resistance. Skinner's Box was not a monster about to swallow her but an adult child ready to leave home, happy to snip the apron strings. She pulled back further and felt the force around her head weaken. She was still a separate and distinct entity. The danger was past. She could not leave yet, though. She had one more thing to do.

She found the thread dealing with sexuality and genetics, and hormones and infertility and libido. Information whirled and twirled. Since she could not decide whether or not she wanted sexuality, she saw no harm in having the most powerful computer in the universe analyze the pros and cons. Lust, fertility. The species. Obsession and fantasies. Estrogen, testosterone. The frontal lobe. Neurons, pituitary gland. Uterus, testicles clitoris, penis. Ovaries.

The heart.

Before her was the solution to reinstating her sexuality. Brain chemistry correctly altered would correct the genes, activate stem cells, spark the production of pheromones, the neurology of desire, and set things right for fertility.

Yes, it made sense.

Just as the computer had originally done to her, she began firing questions at it. Could the solution be applied now? Could the computer send signals to her brain through the cap on her head? Could it affect her neural chemistry?

Yes. It could. With permission, it could use the established communications feedback loop to stimulate the glands necessary to produce the chemicals in the right proportions to elicit the changes. No external application of chemicals or pharmaceuticals was needed; everything required to heal the body was present in it. To instigate the change would take mere nanoseconds. Nanoseconds.

"Answer me, now!" Roach ordered. Annoyed at the interruption, she flicked her fingers.

"Flex your thumb!"

She flexed her thumb. It was all laid out before her; an expanse of interlaced knowledge on human sexuality, so deep and vast it was only the edges she could comprehend. And behind it, among the ongoing calculations, was information on the drug that had done this to her, on Phizenhessen, on Canadian government funding, on her mother's research. Montreal in 2010. Colonel Russell Williams. The demise of the Mafia and a small high-tech company in Kanata, Ontario.

Ah, yes. Someone has already programmed in access to my scrubbed files. She searched the data for evidence of negligence, blame, culpability. The necessary information to ascertain motives and assign guilt was not available.

But you must be able to ascertain motives. You cannot function ethically if you don't know how to do that!

And then it was there, at first just a thin point of light playing across the possible and probable financial, medical and environmental motives behind the research. Most reasons looked pure beneath the brilliant white light. *Or perhaps the light is purifying them.* To effectively deal with the aftermath of these past decisions of unknown origins, the human psyche must—

The word 'understanding' came to mind. Then the light flashed brilliantly like a welder's arc and flooded the entire field of knowledge within her view with one powerful thought—*forgiveness.*

A surge of electrical impulses washed through her brain. Blood rushed to her genitals. Unbearable. She withdrew her hand from Roach's. A convulsion she could not control, arched her back and forced open her eyes.

In the distance, people were hollering. Roach ripped off her cap. Wires clattered to floor. Footsteps clicked frantically across tiles and doors slammed.

Quickly, her muscles relaxed enough for her to turn her head. She strained to see Roach. *I need to let him know I'm okay.*

Roach had both hands high above the computer, about to smash it. "No!" she screamed.

Paul rushed forward, caught Roach's chin with his forearm and sent him back three feet. For a second, Roach teetered there, his hands around his throat and his eyes, wide with pain and anger. Then, one hand still on his throat but the other tensed into a claw, he lunged at Paul, swinging wildly.

"Stop it!" Ladesque cried. "Both of you! Stop it.!"

Paul sidestepped Roach, grasped his shoulder from behind and spun him to the floor. "Would someone get this idiot out of here?" Paul called, looking above him and around the ceiling as if some god might appear to snatch Roach from the planet.

Ladesque swung her feet to the floor and grabbed Paul's arm. "I don't need saving, from either the computer or Roach! If you two can't refrain from behaving like Bohemian warriors, you should both leave!"

A few feet behind Paul, Roach slowly rose. "I'm sorry, Ladesque," he rasped. "Are you okay? You weren't answering my questions."

Paul's jaw dropped. He turned and stared at Roach. "You were asking her questions?"

"Just squeezing my hand," Ladesque intercepted. "I was to squeeze back."

Paul advanced toward Roach and Roach advanced toward him. Neither one showed the least hesitation. "You were not to interfere, Marco! You've broken protocol. I'll have your head."

"Marco?" Ladesque gasped. "Roach, you're Marco? The Marco Rochester who created the mathematical formulas for intelligence?"

Roach ignored her, his attention solely on Paul. "I knew you shouldn't have been trusted. A man who uses a eunuch is indeed not a man."

Ladesque slipped between them. "Enough. Please. Leave this room. Both of you. Fight somewhere else. There's sensitive equipment here, not to mention my dire need to recover…" Ladesque suddenly felt as if she were about to faint.

She eyed up the cot she'd been on. It was six steps away. She might need to make a dive for it. She willed herself to remain steady. She'd finish her sentence, walk steadily away from the men. "I need to recover from what the machine…the machine put me…"

~ * ~

She was somewhere soft but the back of her head throbbed. In the distance, perhaps in another universe, myriad voices were calling her name. Someone was wiping her forehead with a cool cloth and someone's fingers were tapping her palm. American Sign Language: "Are you okay?" She flexed her thumb and opened her eyes. Roach was looking down at her, terror masking his face.

"Are you okay?" Paul asked from the other side of the cot. "You fell, knocked yourself out."

"I'm…I'm—I'm tired. I just want to…sleep."

"No, not now," Paul said sternly. "You must be debriefed. You must…" his voice droned. She was tired. Drained. Exhausted. Exactly like she felt when a migraine passed.

"Ladesque! Speak to me, talk to me. Please. Please don't leave us now. You did so good. Everything went great. Come on, wake up. Ladesque! Roach, move!"

"I'm awake, Paul. I'm fine. I'm just tired. It's an urban myth that those suffering from concussions ought not to be allowed to sleep. A fallacy. I need…to…sleep."

She smelled him, felt his breath on her face. "I'm going to awaken the princess with a kiss." His lips were warm and full. Delicious. "Tell me princess," he said, finally withdrawing. "Did I just do something illegal?"

At her feet, Roach was looking at her with sad eyes. "Don't, Ladesque. Don't let him keep using you."

"He's not using me, Roach," Ladesque said.

"He's been using you since he changed your lab results—"

"You're such a geek," Paul interrupted. "Get out of here. You don't know what you're talking about."

"You were supposed to use someone without libido and ties to the world. That wasn't Ladesque, yet you altered her pheromone results so you could present her to your committee as the sacrificial virgin they were looking for. What's that if not using her?"

"This was her chance to be healed! The computer would repair her genes, make her whole, give her back what chemistry had robbed from her. I wouldn't question my motives if I were you!"

Roach's eyes flicked from Paul to Ladesque and back again. "How—how do you know she needed healing? Didn't her lab results showed she was sexual?"

"Those were just temporary results," Paul said, unaware of the source of Roach's confusion. "Me changing them to zero altered reality very little. She was already rapidly losing the ability to feel the sensations. Another month or two and her levels would all have fallen back to zero."

"But—"

"But if the committee saw positive readings they would have refused her and she would not have had the chance to become whole. Not for a long time, until such computerized treatment had been tested and proven and protocols established. By then it would have been too late. The fourth decade of life is not when one wants to become fertile and amorous."

"Temporary? What's going on here? What's he saying, Ladesque?"

"Roach, you wasted your bribe money on the lab lady. She screwed you over. She didn't have to alter my results to make them positive. They already were. What Paul is saying is true. I've been sexual for the last few months, felt desire and...you know. That kind of stuff. And now, Skinner's Box has made it permanent."

A curtain clouded his eyes; she'd betrayed him. He turned, stuffed his hands in his pant pockets, and slowly walked to the exit.

"Roach, I'm so sorry. Roach!" Ladesque struggled to her feet. She was as dishonest and untrustworthy as he had been—for much lesser reasons. She tossed Paul's hands from her shoulders. "Roach!" He disappeared out the door.

Ladesque ran after him, catching the door just before it closed. She turned. Paul was standing tall and confident. Even in the harsh fluorescent light of the lab he looked beautiful. Symmetric. He was strong. He was aroused. Genetically healthy. He caught her eyes and held them. He wanted her.

Ladesque's nipples hardened and her crotch roared to life. His warm arms about her shoulders, his lips on hers. His throbbing, thick penis filling her empty space.

She opened the door. Thirty feet down the hall, Roach's slumped figure ambled awkwardly and off-center away from her. He'd cuddled her. Protected her. Bought her Canadian beer. He'd risked his career to alter her lab result and risked a gazillion dollar project to communicate with her while she lay helpless at the mercy of the mind machine.

"Roach!" she hollered and took off after him.

He turned as she neared. Tears were streaming down his cheeks. "It's okay, Ladesque. It's fine. Go back to him. You want him, I can tell."

"You've been known to be wrong...Marco." She slipped her hand into his and laid her head on his shoulder. "Unless of course, you're afraid you can't handle a hot-blooded woman with libido?" She snuggled against him. He was soft and warm. He felt so good.

"I'd never be afraid of you, Sally." He stopped and kissed her urgently; he was free to love her and lust her and hold her...and he made sure she knew that. It was a long time before he drew back and gazed into her eyes.

"So, Marco," she said. *Wow, he tastes good.* "Since we both failed all contests so miserably, do you want to forget the tenth floor and join me upstairs as joint master of the God Machine?

Notes from the author

Perhaps we should be more concerned about who's hacking, who's invading, who's spying who's destroying cyberspace than about who's in possession of traditional weapons of mass destruction. But above all, maybe we should be concerned about who is developing the quantum computer.

The truth behind the fiction:

1. There really was a global financial catastrophe that started in 2010 and as of publication of DISPASSIONATE LIES, continues to inflict hardship on many nations, one of the most notorious recently being Greece http://en.wikipedia.org/wiki/Greek_debt_crisis_timeline

2. Canada really did escape the financial collapse basically unscathed... so far.

3. The 2010 Canadian headlines mentioned are true, including the take down of the Montreal Mafia and the Hells Angels, and the murder trial of Colonel Russel William

4. There was a cyber-attack on an Iranian nuclear power plant and suspicions it was computer sabotage that grounded a fleet of F-35 jets http://www.emptywheel.net/2013/02/24/what-if-china-not-just-hacked-but-sabotaged-the-f-35/

5. As of 2014 Edward Snowden and Julian Assange have shown how top-secret data is not safe, how hackers can read, leak and alter digital information, how technology exists to monitor citizens' activities, including through game apps such as Angry Birds. It is my belief if governments can do it; organized crime is doing it, too.

6. The Canadian and US governments did indeed perform secret experiments with mind altering drugs such as LSD on unwitting citizens in the mid-1900's. (Google "Project MKUltra"). As well, it has recently come to light that in the 1940s and 50s the Canadian government approved nutritional experiments on aboriginal children in residential schools. http://www.cbc.ca/news/canada/thunder-bay/aboriginal-nutritional-experiments-had-ottawa-s-approval-1.1404390

7. There are indeed hormones from birth control in our water supply. http://www.scientificamerican.com/article/birth-control-in-water-supply/ Many medications, do indeed, impede libido. An increased risk of some forms of cancer, blood clots, and cardio-vascular disease are

indeed side-effects of present-day oral contraceptives. And infertility rates are rising: http://news.nationalpost.com/2012/02/15/infertility-on-the-rise-in-canada-study/

What state is the web in today? Check out these recent headlines and decide for yourself how secure it is and if there's a link between the unsteady state of cyberspace and global economic uncertainty. Decide for yourself what our world will be like in 2035.

Firewalls, anti-viral programs, and encryption protects me. Right? Dec 29, 2013: **American spies intercept computer deliveries, exploit hardware vulnerabilities, and even hijack Microsoft's internal reporting system to spy on their targets.** http://fw.to/IMC67yi

Who all abuses cyberspace and for what reasons? Oct 09, 2013 **Why would Canada spy on Brazil mining and energy officials?** http://www.cbc.ca/news/politics/why-would-canada-spy-on-brazil-mining-and-energy-officials-1.1931465

What isn't safe from hackers? October 3, 2013 **From Adobe:** *Our investigation currently indicates that the attackers accessed Adobe customer IDs and encrypted passwords on our systems. We also believe the attackers removed from our systems certain information relating to 2.9 million Adobe customers, including customer names, encrypted credit or debit card numbers, expiration dates, and other information relating to customer orders. At this time, we do not believe the attackers removed decrypted credit or debit card numbers from our systems.*

We are also investigating the illegal access to source code of numerous Adobe products. Based on our findings to date, we are not aware of any specific increased risk to customers as a result of this incident. http://helpx.adobe.com/x-productkb/policy-pricing/customer-alert.html

How unstable is the world economy?

Oct 03, 2013: **The Treasury Department warned that a deadlock over raising the nation's debt limit could touch off a new recession even worse than the last one that Americans are still recovering from** http://www.cbc.ca/news/world/u-s-government-shutdown-obama-blames-boehner-1.1894255

October 8, 2013 **Flaherty 'confident' U.S. catastrophe will be averted as IMF revises Canadian growth forecast down** http://www.edmontonjournal.com/business/fp/Flaherty+confident+catastrophe+will+averted+revises+Canadian+growth/9011516/story.html

How widespread is internet abuse? October 1, 2013: **Cybercrime cost Canadians nearly $3.1 billion over the past year http://o. canada.com/technology/internet/cybercrime/**
We can only guess who's to blame for disrupting communications… repeatedly: Sep 28, 2013: **Shaw phone service mostly restored around Alberta Service went down Saturday morning across Alberta and Ontario** http://www.cbc.ca/news/canada/calgary/shaw-phone-service-down-around-alberta-1.1872067

Transportation September 17 2013: **Porter flights cancelled due to computer outages** http://www.cbc.ca/news/canada/toronto/porter-flights-cancelled-due-to-computer-outages-1.1858520

Is anything safe? Published 2012 by International Atomic Energy Agency: **Computer Security at Nuclear Facilities** http://www-pub. iaea.org/books/IAEABooks/8927/Computer-Security-at-Nuclear-Facilities-Chinese-Edition

Has the Cold War turned cyber? August 30, 2013: **Why the U.S. Should Use Cyber Weapons Against Syria** http://www.defenseone. com/technology/2013/08/why-us-should-use-cyber-weapons-against-syria/69776/?oref=d-channelriver

The young know the ropes, but do the ones in power? September 16 2013 The military is recruiting middle school hackers http:// www.businessinsider.com/the-military-is-recruiting-middle-school-hackers-2013-9

But seriously, what does Canada have to do with anything of importance on the world stage? http://www.cbc.ca/news/politics/ snowden-document-shows-canada-set-up-spy-posts-for-nsa-1.2456886 The briefing notes make it clear Canada plays a very robust role in intelligence-gathering around the world in a way that has won respect from its American equivalents.

Can human consciousness really be digitized? http://www.pbs.org/ wgbh/nova/next/physics/physicists-say-consciousness-might-be-a-state-of-matter/

About the Author

Eileen Schuh lives in the remote northern boreal forests of Alberta, Canada. Drawing inspiration from the wilderness, she creates entire universes populated with fascinating characters doing intriguing things.

Her interest in psychology dates back decades to her years as a psychiatric nurse. Her penchant for pondering Quantum Physics came later, when she needed something to contemplate while her hands were busy with the many repetitive and boring tasks of motherhood.

Schuh recently retired from a life of careers that varied from nurse to journalist to editor to business woman. She remains active in her adopted community of St. Paul and basks in the love and loyalty of family and friends. There's no doubt, however, that it's her grandchildren who are now the centre of her universe.

More mind bending Science Fiction from WolfSinger Publications

Aqua Vitae – Therese Arkenberg

Jenes Inarya wants to experience everything. And quite frankly, she doesn't think she can live life to the fullest in the time she's been allotted. A search through lore and legend from the Eight Immortals of Chinese myth to the Garden of Eden finally leads her to what she seeks--across the galaxy, to the planet of Arak, which possesses an immortal ecosystem. By eating food prepared from the immortal plants of Arak, Jenes can alter her metabolism and gain eternal life. In her case, it's a cup of palm wine. A real aqua vitae.

But the prospect of eternal life quickly causes more problems than it solves.

Claire – Sally Kuntz

It was an open and shut case of someone's reckless actions that had killed his sister. Mark knows that, and he is going to expose the group responsible for the wild, headlong, daredevils they are. But Mark has a lot to learn; about the killer and about himself.

Mark arrives on Eire's moon with a complete set of beliefs: it hadn't been his sister's fault in any way, the person responsible for shooting down his sister's ship, the group the killer belongs to are reckless scum, and he will right the situation by exposing them in print. But the longer he stays the less his beliefs apply.

Remember Me to Paradise – Amy Benesch

A Shapeshifter from a planet known as Paradise, comes to Earth on a mission to rescue other Shapeshifters who may have become trapped in Earth shapes and are unable to return to their home planet.

During his time on Earth the Shapeshifter becomes a dog, a duck, a pigeon, a human male, and a human female. It is as a human female that Shapeshifter begins to forget its true identity. She goes to a therapist who urges her to write down her dreams.

Although her dreams terrify her (she can't understand why she dreams of flying and of making love to women), she keeps working to put the pieces of the puzzle together and recover her memory, although with each passing day she becomes more identified with her current shape and less likely to believe the truth of who she really is.

Schrodinger's Cat – Eileen Schuh

Chordelia, straddling two of the realities proposed in Everett's Many Worlds Theory of Quantum Physics, has no idea how distorted the line is between choice and fate.

In one of her worlds, Chorie's young daughter is dying—a drama that quickly contaminates her other, much rosier, reality. Before long, the emotional burden of dealing with two separate lives spawns heated legal battles, endangers her role as mother and wife, and causes people in both universes to judge her insane. As her lives begin to crumble, so does Chorie's heart and mind.

When Dr. Penny, a man with disturbing, murky, hypnotic eyes offers to rid her of the life that's causing so much pain, she must decide if she is willing to sacrifice the chance to be with her dying child for the chance to save her marriage and experience happiness.

She thinks she's planned it well—she's researched her choices, prepared herself for the consequences, put everything in place. She makes her decision. However....

Life, as it has the propensity to do, strikes back with the dark and unexpected.

Check them out at www.wolfsingerpubs.com

www.ingramcontent.com/pod-product-compliance
Lightning Source LLC
Chambersburg PA
CBHW060747180626
46818CB00002B/481